ACCLAIM FOR NELSON NYE

"The ace writer of Western fiction."

— Boston *Post*

"Nye's gift for authentic detail, real cowpuncher lingo, suspense and unflagging excitement make him one of the best in the business."

— Dallas *Morning News*

"One of the great masters of Western fiction!"

— NW Arkansas *Times*

"An expert at Western tales."

— Atlanta *Journal*

"Marvelous command of Western lingo, salty humor and real characters."

— Los Angeles *Times*

"Mr. Nye really knows his horses and his books are distinguished among Westerns by authoritative background and dialogue."

— Pasadena *Star-News*

"Nye is always above average."

— Los Angeles *Examiner*

"One of the best contemporary Western writers."

— Chattanooga *Times*

NO PLACE TO HIDE

by Nelson Nye

NO PLACE TO HIDE

NELSON NYE

PaperJacks LTD.

TORONTO   NEW YORK

AN ORIGINAL

PaperJacks

NO PLACE TO HIDE

PaperJacks LTD

330 STEELCASE RD. E., MARKHAM, ONT. L3R 2M1
210 FIFTH AVE., NEW YORK, N.Y. 10010

First edition published April 1988

ISBN 0-7701-0882-2
Copyright © 1988 by Nelson Nye
All rights reserved
Printed in the USA

For
John Douglas
with much appreciation
from
The Baron

Chapter One

Behind him on the road up from Mexico the heat hung in a shimmering haze, curling and writhing like a drift of smoke against the blue-gray hills. Wishbone Reilly, gaunt as a half-starved timber wolf, crested a rise on his dun-colored mule and pulled up for a breather.

Big boned and florid, Reilly was a sandy-haired galoot. His frequently patched shirt and Mexican pantalones had been snagged by brush and were in little better shape than the scuffed and scratched Hyer boots that covered his outsized feet. On his head was a once-black battered old Gammage hat now faded by the sun to a dingy gray.

There was a war on in Mexico but this had nothing to do with his haste to get out of here. A long-forgotten great uncle on his mother's side had left him both a ranch and a mine a whoop and a holler from Tombstone, and for a ranny who'd spent ten grubstaked years hunting the elusive pot of gold, this looked like a fortune and he was anxious to get at it.

He'd been called a fool to waste the best years of his life in the burning wastes of Sonora, a part of Mexico mainly inhabited by Indios, banditos and several tribes of rattlesnakes, not a few of which got around on two legs. Hell, a man was more to be pitied, he thought, than scorned, for clinging to cherished illusions like a hard-held belief in justice for all and every man getting his just deserts.

He wasn't sure the meek — like it said in the Good Book — would be inheriting the earth for some while yet. But Reilly's flagging belief in a beneficent Providence had certainly perked up when that lawyer feller at Hermosillo had unexpectedly told him about Uncle Cornelious and his gift of Bullybueno, one of the finest spreads in all Arizona!

Forty-three hundred acres — a good part of them in grass — a year-round stream, twenty-seven windmills with dug tanks alongside, over a hundred head of horses, and cows beyond count. Nothing there to be sneezed at. Damn near big as the whole state of Delaware.

If you let yourself go, it could make a feller feel like a dad-blamed plutocrat!

"Of course," the lawyer had mentioned, "with your uncle being so long away, the place may seem a bit seedy at the moment, but you can put that to rights with a little work and diligence."

Uncle Cornelious, it appeared, had coddled an inclination to examine the far sides of a good many hills in distant parts, and he seemed more interested in adventures than in any profit these journeys might bring him. "A great one for moving on," the lawyer said. It had been the proceeds of one of Uncle Cornelious's adventures which had allowed him on a whim to acquire Bullybueno. Once he'd got it fixed to his liking, he was off again, leaving a three-man caretaker crew to look after things and keep the spread going.

Wishbone guessed he could scrape up enough money

to fill out the crew and put in order whatever needed fixing. And there was that mine, of course.

Seemed like the lawyer might have had some reservations on that subject. "Yes, well," he'd said, "I gathered the mine had never been recorded. Kept the crew at the far edge of things whenever he felt like going underground. A rather secretive man, your uncle, not one to put a great deal of trust even in his lawyer. For instance, he gave me neither the mine's location nor directions for finding it. He did say it was silver, incredibly rich . . . great chunks of pure silver, some big around as a washtub. Inside your acreage was all he would tell me."

That didn't bother Wishbone too much. With ten years of prospecting behind him, he reckoned if it was there he would find it. No doubt about that!

So here he was, within sixty miles of this grand inheritance. He had the deed plus $700 from the Hermosillo bank. All he had to do now was ride in and take possession. He guessed, having gotten out of Mexico with his skin still intact, he might as well give Rachel, his dun-colored mule, a night of well-deserved rest and himself a decent bed. Tombstone wasn't more than five miles away and would afford him a chance to make a few discrete inquiries.

It was the shank of the afternoon when Wishbone reached town and left Rachel at the West End Livery. He popped into the Alhambra to lubricate his whistle. Tired of being served like a common *paisano* at the bar, Reilly took a table off in one corner and waited for service. Not much point in being a *rico* without the respect and privileges commonly accorded a gentleman, he decided. So let 'em come wait on him.

The female who finally came for his order was a brassy-haired blonde with skinny legs but enough up top to supply two ordinary dames, not to mention a pair of nipples that stuck out like bullets. A younger, black-haired girl was at the next table eating what looked like a Spanish omelet. Gesturing toward it, Reilly said, "I'll have the same with refried beans and a bottle of José Cuervo, *por favor*."

After the buxom waitress had departed with his order, Wishbone discovered his black-haired neighbor examining him with interest. Blushing as she glanced away, she picked up her fork and went on with her meal. But as soon as Wishbone ceased his scrutiny, he could feel her eyes on him again. Deciding what was sauce for the goose was just as good for the gander, he began ogling her in earnest.

She was a bundle of contrasts. Her gypsy finery was pretty much in rags. Her big-eyed childlike face had a look of shy innocence which was only enhanced by those painful blushes. He guessed she was barely sixteen until he noticed how well she was put together.

Been a long while since he'd found himself this close to such a tempting armful. He was trying to think how to strike up a conversation when she said with just the right touch of childish temerity, "Are you a refugee too, Señor?"

Despite her tattered clothes she did not look to be the offspring of peons. Her features were too fine, too pale when she wasn't flushed up like a flaming sunset. "Guess you might say that," he told her. "Been down there prospectin' these last several years, but it wasn't the troubles that pushed me out. How about you?"

"It was terrible," she said with a delectable shudder. "My father owned a great hacienda until the rebels came and killed everyone they could find. With the aid of the Virgin, I managed to escape. Hiding by day, moving only at night, it took me almost a month to get up here — which was only yesterday."

"What are you going to do?"

"Well, Rockin'-Chair Emma, the owner of this place,

has offered me a job . . . but I don't know. You should see the things she expects me to wear!"

With his eyes on her blushing cheeks, Wishbone nodded. "Can you cook?"

"That isn't what she has in mind. She wants me to —" Breaking off she said, "Here comes Birdy O'Shay with your food, Señor."

The buxom blonde put a heaping plate down in front of him along with the tumbler-capped bottle he'd ordered and went flouncing off behind the bar. "Moves like a battleship," Reilly mumbled, and the girl managed a tentative answering smile.

"You takin' the job?"

"I suppose I'll have to. I . . . I have no money."

"Can you cook? I mean Mexican food? I got a ranch about sixty miles from here. Out back of beyond."

Her eyes hid again behind those long lashes and her cheeks flushed once more.

Reilly, catching her thought, hastened to reassure her. "I'm in need of a housekeeper is what I had in mind. Could pay you forty a month."

Seeing her hesitation and the suspicion in her eyes, he said, "You wouldn't be cookin' for the hands, just for me and yourself."

"You have servants, Señor?"

"Don't imagine so. I just inherited this spread from my mother's uncle — haven't seen it yet. Figured to get out there tomorrow. Just a caretaker crew out there right now."

"You expect me to sleep with you?"

"Good lord, no!" It was Reilly's cheeks that were on fire now. "Just get my meals an' keep the place lookin' shipshape. Aside from that you'll be your own boss."

Suddenly inspired he hustled to point out, "Be a lot nicer than bein' all the time pawed by the roughnecks in this place."

"I . . . I would have to think about it."

"That's okay. My name's Reilly — Wishbone Reilly. What's yours?"

"Ronero. I am called Chacha, though my given name is Earnestina."

"Chacha Ronero — makes a mighty pretty sound. You think it over. Take all the time you want. I'm stabled at the West End Livery and puttin' up at the Aztec House. If you decide to come with me be at the livery by six tomorrow morning."

Next step, he reckoned, was to see the sheriff whose name, he'd been told, was Harold Burton. "Stranger here?" his informant asked. When Reilly nodded, the man said, "This time of the day you'll be most likely to find him at the Occidental."

"Next to the Alhambra?" Reilly frowned since he'd just come from there.

"That's right. Allen Street, between Fourth and Fifth. If he isn't there, try the Oriental on the corner of Fifth."

Wishbone thanked him and set off, trying to decide how much of his business he ought to divulge. The Alhambra seemed to be one of the better-class saloons, more like a gentleman's club than the general run of drink emporiums, handsomely furnished in a kind of quiet splendor. He told the nearest barkeep he was looking for Harold Burton, and the apron said, "You just missed him. Try the Oriental."

The Oriental, at the corner of Fifth and Allen, seemed a shade more elegant than the place he'd just left. More mirrors, more oil paintings, better fixtures. The barkeep said, "Burton? That's him over at the corner table talking to Morgan Earp."

Wishbone went over there. "Can I buy you gents a drink," he asked when the seated pair glanced up at him.

"What for?" said the bigger of the two.

"Well, as a sort of friendly gesture to celebrate the acquaintance."

"Didn't know we were acquainted."

Wishbone grinned. "Maybe we should be. Name's Wishbone Reilly. I'm the new owner of Bullybueno. Just stopped by to make myself known and ask directions."

The slighter man stood up and put his hand out, giving Reilly's a good firm clasp. "I'm Sheriff Burton and this here's Morgan Earp, Wyatt's brother."

Wyatt's brother nodded, not bothering to get up or stick out his paw. "Did I understand you to say you own Bullybueno?"

"That's right. Inherited it from my great uncle, Cornelious O'Neal."

"Cornelious, eh? So the old coot finally kicked off. Some might tell you it was considerable overdue."

Seeing the glint in Reilly's eye, Harold Burton said, "Pull up a chair and rest your haunches. What are you figuring to do with the place?"

"Live there, I suppose, and work it. If you mean am I thinkin' of selling, the answer is no. Understand my uncle thought a heap of that place."

"Well," Burton said after exchanging a look with Earp, "you won't have no trouble finding the spread. Straight west of town. Matter of fifty-eight miles or thereabouts. Says Bullybueno over the gate."

Wishbone beckoned the barkeep. Earp got up and wandered off. "What's the matter with that feller?" Reilly asked the sheriff. "He always that rude?"

"Got somethin' on his mind, I guess. I'll have whatever you're drinkin'."

"Couple shots of Old Crow." When they came, Wishbone said, "Here's mud in your eye."

Putting down his jigger, Burton said, "You look like a man who's spent some time in the desert. Ever done any ranching?"

"Brought up on a ranch, but that was some while ago. Spent the last ten years prospectin'. Four . . . five of 'em down in Sonora."

"Damn hot country," Burton observed. "You've got papers, I suppose."

"You bet. Right here," Wishbone affirmed, slapping the buttoned pocket of his patched-up shirt.

"When'd you last see your uncle?"

"Must've been twenty years anyway. I didn't know nothin' about inheritin' the ranch till his lawyer at Hermosillo got hold of me."

"Mind if I look at them?"

Reilly got the papers out of his pocket and put them on the table. The sheriff looked them over and passed them back. "Yep," he said, "reckon she's yours right enough. When you goin' out there?"

"Figured to leave first thing in the morning."

Burton seemed to be turning something over in his mind, but all he said was, "Been nice knowin' you. Good luck — and thanks for the drink."

Wishbone Reilly arrived at the West End Livery at ten minutes to six, got his mule out of hock and stood around waiting for the girl. When it was twenty past the hour and she still hadn't showed, he climbed into the saddle and went hunting for her. Then he recalled her saying she had come here afoot, had hiked out of Mexico on Shank's mare.

She was eating a breakfast of bacon, eggs, toast and java. He got a tremulous smile. Curbing his impatience, but being a take-charge sort of hombre, he said, "I'll go fetch you a mule and meet you outside the front door — and here's some change to pay for your grub." He put it down on the table and headed for the batwings.

"I'm not sure I ought to go out there," she murmured. "Supposing I find doing your housekeeping doesn't suit me?"

"I can't think why it wouldn't."

"I'm not looking for charity."

"You're not gettin' it either. I want that house to feel like a home," Reilly said and pushed through the batwings.

He was back in a quarter of an hour with a brown mule in tow to find her waiting as expected. Just herself, in the same rags, and no luggage. Wishbone helped her into the saddle, got into his own, clucked to Rachel and led off at a trot, taking it for granted she would be right behind him.

"Does this job mean I get an extra dress?"

That did fetch his head around. "Glad you mentioned it." Considering a moment, he told her gruffly, "You'll get anything you need." They backtracked to the One Price House, which sold clothing, next to the Oriental Saloon. "Better get a couple while you're at it," he said and gave her some currency without bothering to count it.

A few minutes later she came out with a bandbox and would have handed him what was left of his money except he waved it away, telling her to keep it. Then he helped her remount and, hitching her cardboard box to her saddle, he got into his own. Once more they began the trek out of town.

Once they got through the hills they were into the open desert. Fortunately, Wishbone thought, she had purchased a sensible wide-brimmed hat. Considering the fact that the sun was turning up the temperature pretty near to where it would fry things, it seemed a pretty smart acquisition. The glare was atrocious. All the jackrabbits had taken to their holes or were crouched under bushes. The only moving things they could see, save for twisters and an occasional mirage, were a couple of roadrunners that had apparently decided to amble west with them.

Along toward noon Wishbone handed her a couple of

strips of jerky to chew on. She guessed they were making pretty good time, for Reilly, cavalry fashion, was alternating the pace between walking and trotting at half hour intervals. But in this oppressive heat the hours seemed to drag interminably. The scenery failed to hold her interest. It was practically identical to what she'd known back in Mexico.

Mostly she rode in silence, keeping her thoughts to herself. These revolved almost exclusively around her benefactor, this gaunt scarecrow of a gringo who was taking her to God knew where. She worried some about this, but surely, she thought, it would be better than what she'd been offered by Rockin'-Chair Emma.

Finally they reached the gate with the name Bullybueno burnt into a board nailed to the crosspiece. But it seemed just more of the same. Not a building was in sight, just a lane leading north toward distant hills that looked faintly blue in the intense light and heat.

"Not long now," Reilly said, grinning back at her.

Cramped and exhausted, she prayed it would not be.

Dusk was already beginning to set in when, topping a hill, they found the buildings of Bullybueno spread out below them, a solitary light showing from a window of the main house. Built of plastered adobe, it resembled most of southern Arizona's buildings. It was flat-roofed with narrow slits for windows and had a somewhat pretentious bell tower.

Wishbone, taking in this view of his inheritance, let out a great sigh. "Home at last," he remarked in a tone of vast satisfaction and rode down the slope and into the hot, barren yard.

Before he had even got near the house he saw a man with a rifle come off the veranda. "Lookin' for somebody?"

"Nope," said Reilly. "I'm the new owner. Just heired

this spread from my Uncle Cornelious. Why the artillery? You got Indian troubles?"

Twisting his head instead of answering, the fellow yelled back at the house, "Hey, boss! Come see what just rode in!"

"What's that?" a gruff voice called from the house.

"Feller in the yard here says he's the heir." He chucked a grin at Reilly. "Looks like he's fixin to move in," he called back. "Got his woman with him."

Just as Chacha reined her mule to a stop another man came out of the shadows off to the right to stand at her elbow. "Mex'kin tamale," he growled at the first man, ogling her. "New owner's wearin' Mex'kin pants."

Now a tall man strode onto the veranda. Puffing a cigar, he stood looking them over. He wore a white hat with a rattlesnake band and was expensively garbed in a ranch-style store-bought suit. Pant legs stuffed into shiny green boots, he sported big-roweled spurs. "My name's Hannigan. Who the hell are you?"

"Wishbone Reilly —"

"Then you better start wishin' you'd never heard of this place because there ain't no heir. I'm the owner of Bullybueno."

"Must be some mistake —"

The man with the cigar sticking out of his face said, "No mistake. Grab him, boys."

Before Reilly could think what was happening he was yanked from the saddle. While he was trying to catch his balance somebody's fist exploded in his face and he couldn't see anything but a shower of sparks as someone latched on to his arms from behind and a second hay-maker slammed into his belly. As he doubled over, a knee took him under the chin like a battering ram, straightening him up for another fist to the gut. From there on he lost count.

A bucket of water dumped on his head brought him round. Before he could get anything in focus he was dragged to his feet to face the cigar-smoking man — the one. who'd called himself Hannigan — who still stood on the veranda.

Hannigan said, "Around here, Reilly, possession's the biggest end of the law, and on Bullybueno we generally take care of that from a holster. Just count yourself lucky. You show up here again and you'll get a slug an' just enough ground to cover you over."

Neither expecting an answer, nor getting one, he said, "Drape that fool over his jackass, Benson, and tell his woman to get him out of here. On the double!"

Soon as Benson flopped him belly down across the saddle with a piggin string joining wrists to ankles, Hannigan stepped off the veranda with a spoke he'd kicked from the railing. This he smashed viciously across Rachel's rump.

Chapter Two

Even with the Blessed Virgin's help, Chacha Ronero thought, she would never be able to keep this gringo aboard his mule long enough to reach a place of comparative safety. In Mexico there were hundreds of tiny villages; here, in all the miles they had traveled, there was not one house or person. Tombstone might as well have been on the moon for any chance they had of reaching it, and with no help nearer, what was she to do?

He looked half dead already, and if he ever slipped off his precarious perch, even if the mule did not go crazy and bolt, she would never be able to get him back up there.

By the time they began to climb into the hills Chacha was nearly exhausted by her continual efforts to keep Wishbone on the saddle. If only the man would come to his senses, perhaps he'd be able to tell her what to do.

They were deep into the hills when in a whisper she

could scarcely hear he gasped, "Stop — this motion is killing me . . ."

Scrambling out of her saddle, she ran to his side. "Jackknife . . . in pocket," he muttered. "Cut me loose."

"There is nothing in your pockets — they took everything you had."

It took an unconscionable while for this to get through to him. Finally he mumbled, "Untie . . . knots."

If he had not been in such a pitiable state, she guessed she could never have managed. Already from the jolting he was half off the saddle. With the piggin string off his swollen wrists and ankles he fell to the ground as though spilled from a sack.

The only light came from distant stars and was far too dim for her to see the look on his face. For one awful moment she thought he had died, but then her hand found his chest and discovered his heart was still beating.

Crossing herself and feeling not quite so desperate, she led both mules into the brush and tied them.

"Where are we?" Reilly said suddenly. "An' how long have we been here?"

"Three days," she replied, bending over him. "How do you feel?"

"Weak as a kitten. Where are we?" he repeated.

"Still in the hills that are nearest your ranch."

"Have I been out of my head all this time?"

"No. You came and went."

He made an effort to raise himself on an elbow and fell back with a gasp, both eyes shut. Presently, opening them, he said, "You must have had your hands full."

She did not go into that. "I know something of herbs. There was jerky in your saddlebags and I managed to shoot a rabbit with your rifle."

"You must be starved."

"I got the saddles off the mules. They've been eating brush. I was afraid to turn them loose."

"Rachel won't run off . . ."

His eyes closed again and he slept. That evening Chacha shot another rabbit. Next morning he announced that he was much better and, with her help and a few stifled groans, managed to get to his feet. Feeling rather wobbly but strong enough to stand, he said, "Tonight we've got to get out of here."

Rachel came to him when he whistled that evening, the brown mule tagging along in her wake. Chacha saddled them both. When Reilly was mounted he handed him his rifle, the sixteen-shot Henry, which he balanced across his lap. "Reckon I look like hell warmed over," he muttered as she climbed aboard her mule.

Despite the herbs and her many ministrations, he didn't look much like he had when she'd first seen him in Tombstone's Alhambra Saloon. She said encouragingly, "To me you look fine."

"Guess I look like Joseph's coat. If it wasn't for you, I'd probably be dead."

Traveling by easy stages, it took them two days to get back to town where, with some of the money saved from her shopping, the girl got them rooms at the American Hotel.

Reilly, still stiff and aching, decided it was time to pay the sheriff another visit. He found the jail at 230 Toughnut Street, which was on the east side one block south of the town's main road. Burton was in his office in the front part of the building. The sheriff eyed him impassively. "Well," he said, "I see you've been out there."

Wishbone gave him a twisted grin. "Those fellers play rough. I came out of there belly down across my saddle with Hannigan's promise of just enough ground to cover me next time I showed."

The sheriff nodded soberly. "I can see you figure to afford him an opportunity."

"Took everything I had on me, some six hundred and fifty bucks and all my papers. Damn good thing you had a look at them."

Burton considered him from under raised brows. "Don't see how that'll be of much help."

Wishbone could feel the bile rising in him. "You're goin' to stay out of this?"

Burton said, "Out of my jurisdiction. You might talk to Wyatt Earp. He's deputy U.S. marshal here." He cleared his throat. "You can tell him I've seen your papers, that I acknowledge you the rightful owner."

Reilly scowled. "Where'll I find him?" he demanded.

"Don't know. Was sitting in a high-stakes game at the Oriental last night. Might still be goin' on."

"You're a hell of a sheriff."

Burton showed a wry smile. "I've been called worse names. Point is your ranch is twenty miles out of my legitimate territory. Like everyone else in a public office, I have a set of rules —"

Reilly was too mad to wait for the rest of it. Storming out of the place without another word, he strode up Fifth Street to Allen, feeling more riled with every step, and went elbowing his way through the swinging doors and into the Oriental bar.

At this time of day there weren't many customers with a foot on the rail. Only one apron was back of the bar, a heavyset man with a protruding paunch. The little hair he had left was tastefully curled across his forehead. "Boys," he said, "this here's Wishbone Reilly, heir to Bullybueno."

The row of heads turned. A few of them nodded before turning back to things of more interest. His face darkening, Wishbone demanded, "Where'll I find Wyatt Earp about now?"

The barkeep glanced at the clock. "Probably settin' around shootin' the breeze with Doc Holiday."

Reilly presently ran Earp to earth in Billy King's saloon. He was at a table near the back with a rather slender gent in frock coat and string tie. Pulling up alongside their table, Wishbone said when Earp looked up, "If it ain't inconvenient, I'd like a few words with you on a matter of business."

"If it's law business, son, you go right ahead."

By this time, after mulling over his injuries, Wishbone was into a pretty sod-pawing mood. He told about inheriting his uncle's ranch, described his reception at Bullybueno and stood waiting for Earp to make some comment.

The deputy U.S. marshal promptly obliged. "Yes," he said, "that's enough to steam anyone up. Looks like they worked you over pretty good. If it was in my power, I'd go clear them rascals off your place. What they done, however, ain't a federal offense. Afraid that's the long an' short of it, Reilly."

"Well, by God," Wishbone said, "you needn't think I'm goin' to set back an' take it!"

"You want to be a little careful," Earp told him. "From what I hear that Hannigan's a pretty nasty specimen. Them fellers your uncle left in charge of the place sort of plain disappeared. Ain't hide nor hair of any of 'em been seen since this Hannigan took over out there."

Gnawing on his mustache Earp considered Reilly thoughtfully. "You have to kill anyone, son, you make mighty sure the bodies stay buried. That's the best advice I can give you."

Chapter Three

Next morning Wishbone went around to Brown's Bank with an introductory note from the sheriff, who described Reilly as the rightful heir to Bullybueno. He was treated with courtesy, but the bank, or at least the gentleman he spoke with, did not have sufficient confidence in Wishbone's prospects to make him the loan he so badly needed.

He went over to the Oriental for a talk with Mike Joyce, the proprietor, who told him bluntly: "Lots of folks round here would make you a loan — and be glad to do it, if you had possession. The hard fact is you haven't, and Hannigan's not the kind any sensible man would care to have for an enemy."

Wishbone went back to Rockin'-Chair Emma's and proceeded to tie one on. Once he was thoroughly drunk he said a number of things he would not have had he been sober.

When he finally returned to his room at the American Hotel, Chacha eyed him with considerable dismay. "You will not get your ranch back by becoming a *borrachón*. I know of nothing more disgusting than having to listen to a drunk. Go away," she said, and shut the door in his face.

Giving IOUs right and left to pay for his booze, Wishbone managed to stay drunk for a week. Ejected from his room at the American Hotel and likewise barred from the premises of the West End Livery, whose proprietor wanted no crazy drunks roosting in his loft, he had no idea where — or even if — he had slept during this bender. When his promisory notes no longer sufficed to keep him in liquor and Burton put him in jail to keep him off the streets, he finally sobered up. After which the sheriff, like a Dutch uncle, brought Wishbone face to face with a few hard facts. "If you're determined to make a fool of yourself go and do it somewhere else. You've made yourself a nuisance long enough around here. Either straighten up and act like a man or get out of this town and stay out."

It took a couple more days to get his wits to working. After which, in some fashion he was never quite sure of, he found himself in the company of a villainous-looking rascal who answered to the name of Ives Hannah, an hombre with a patch over one eye, who swaggered around with a gun on each hip. "You wanta git Bully-bueno back, you're gonna need some help and I'm just the feller to find it for you," Hannah told him.

"Sorry, pal. I got no money an' no damn credit."

"Don't need any. Just leave it to me," Hannah said with a wink. "I know just the boys you need for that business."

"What boys?" Reilly said, considering him through bloodshot eyes.

"Friends of mine. Make me ramrod of your ranch an' I'll get you a crew."

Reilly looked at him dubiously. "When? And what's it goin' to cost me?"

"Meet you at the Dividend Saloon, eight o'clock tomorrow mornin'. I'll have the crew an' when you're established we'll talk about compensation. Okay?"

Wishbone nodded. He couldn't see that he had anything to lose. "All right," he growled, "but just remember I'm the boss."

Reilly turned up at the Dividend next morning promptly at eight to find Hannah waiting with the promised crew. "Boys," Hannah said in an unctuous voice, "shake hands with your new boss, Wishbone Reilly, the gent who rightfully owns Bullybueno." The four men turned out to be named Jim Cheek, Frosty, Bean Belly and Flash Stegman. A tough-looking assortment, Wishbone thought, and then reminded himself he was in no position to pick and choose.

Introductions taken care of, Hannah said, "Let's go —"

"Just a minute," Reilly interrupted, catching hold of his arm. "You got any idea how to get those buggers out of there?"

"You bet," the black-patched Hannah said and grinned broadly. "You just leave it to me an' by this time tomorrer you'll be the lord of all you survey."

With a jingle of spur chains and creaking saddle leather the group headed west like a cavalry column, Hannah riding next to the heir at the front.

For about a half hour they rode without speaking. Finally, unable to contain his curiosity, Wishbone said, "Don't you figure I ought to be put in the picture?" Ives Hannah simply chuckled. "You're in it, boss — right up there, front and center."

"I mean," Wishbone said, "I want to know what you've got in mind."

"No hurry about that. You'll see when we git there."

"That's not good enough. I want to know now," Reilly said with some asperity.

Hannah twisted his head to glance behind him. His villainous face looked hacked from granite. "This is my show, boss. Each of them rannies knows his part an' has been picked to perform it — savvy? Less you know before you see it pulled off the better you're goin' to be pleased with the outcome."

Reilly was beginning to have second thoughts about the whole thing and particularly about the caliber of the men he was riding with. He'd been feeling pretty desperate and very hung over when he'd accepted Hannah's proposition, thinking he'd already hit rock bottom and nothing could get worse; now he wasn't so sure. But he consoled himself with the thought that once established as the acknowledged owner of Bullybueno he could damn well do as he pleased about this scurvy crew. But after all, sometimes it took fire to fight fire and, as Wyatt Earp had told him, so long as the bodies never came to light he would be in the clear. He only hoped the marshal knew what he was talking about.

No matter how hard he tried, Wishbone could not quite banish the uneasiness he felt about employing such a rough-looking outfit. Another thing that fed his uneasiness was the extreme likelihood that any allegiance felt by these men would be to Hannah, who'd recruited them, not to himself.

The trip this time was just as long as it had been the first time he'd covered this ground, but it seemed to become considerably more arduous as he considered the probable character of his companions. They didn't look the kind of men he'd want to meet in any alley.

Ives Hannah seemed in no great hurry to get to the Bullybueno. For the most part, except for an occasional gallop, he kept the pace to a leisurely walk, which gave Reilly the notion he'd no intention of arriving before nightfall. It occurred to him Hannah might have scouted the ground before approaching him.

The sun slipped down out of sight just as they came

into the last batch of hills. Hannah looked at him and said, "I've got this all set up and you're not to take any part in it — okay?"

Wishbone nodded. "Suits me," he said.

"Good. This way your conscience will be clear if there's a hitch."

When they reached the last crest Hannah called a halt to their progress and they stayed down out of sight until it was completely dark. At this point Hannah said, "Hand your reins to Reilly, Jim; he'll be holding the horses. Go ahead now. You've got fifteen minutes."

As soon as Jim Cheek, the Indian, disappeared the rest grabbed their rifles, got out of their saddles and began working their way over the crest. Soon they were out of Wishbone's sight, and with the five horses' reins firmly gripped, Reilly moved in the same direction, still in the saddle, until he could see the lamplit windows below.

He was pretty keyed up. His throat felt drier than a sunbaked boot. He couldn't help wondering what it was the Indian had been sent off to do. He thought the fifteen minutes must have long since passed, and still nothing happened. The whole scene looked peaceful as a mother cow cleaning up a brand-new calf.

Then, off some way behind the squat shape of the bunkhouse, he saw a curl of flame about where the barn should be, watched it waver and brighten, climb higher and widen. Then he plainly heard someone shout, "Fire!"

Running men burst from the bunkhouse, and Wishbone heard the sound of rifles. Two men fell headlong, another spun half around. A fourth had almost got himself out of the light of the flames when he was sent sprawling. A hard-ridden horse left the back of the main house. There were yells, more rifle fire. Then the flames disappeared and Hannah's shout sailed across the yard: "Hustle them horses down here, Reilly!"

Chapter Four

Praying to God that it hadn't been Hannigan who'd escaped, Wishbone went over the crest, leading his five horses at a smart lope. But Hannah's tone of voice had set his back up. It seemed like Hannah had already forgotten who was boss. There was a scowl on Wishbone's face as he rode up to the Bullybueno and flung down the reins in front of the black-patched foreman.

Hannah, paying him no mind at all, ordered Frosty and Bean Belly into their saddles with a terse command to fetch back Hannigan. Then he came wheeling round, a twisted grin on his face to inform the heir that, as promised yesterday, Bullybueno was his to have and to hold.

"Didn't expect you to burn down my barn!"

"Hell, it ain't scarcely singed," Hannah flung back at him. "That blaze wasn't nothin' but a couple bales of straw I had the Indian set afire to give us a target when Hannigan's crew piled outa the bunkhouse. Worked, didn't it?"

Not bothering to answer, Reilly strode off to have a look at his barn. He found that Hannah was right. The barn was intact, but that didn't excuse the man's insolence. Something would have to be done about Hannah. And, he thought, Earp's advice on his mind as he looked around, something would have to be done about these cadavers. But not yet, he decided. Considering Hannah's cocky attitude, these were not problems to be rushed into. They were likely to require considerable thought.

He went back to the others, thinking he wanted Chacha out here to put the house in order and cook him up some good Spanish meals. But with no cash in his pockets and these bastards on the premises, he couldn't afford to go after her himself, not with a round trip of better than a hundred miles staring at him. And who could he trust to fetch her here safely — even if she'd permit herself to be alone with one of them?

Life might be better he thought, but it was sure getting more complicated hour by hour! Stifling a sigh, he said to Hannah, "You better post a couple hands in them hills to make sure that bugger don't catch us off guard."

The black-patched face showed its nasty grin. "I don't get caught off guard. And if you're talkin' about Hannigan, you're kickin' up a mountain out of a mole hill. If he manages to git away from them boys —"

"Post two hands in them hills right now," Wishbone ordered, stopping Hannah in midsentence.

After a sharp glance Hannah said, "Sure thing, boss." He sent Jim Cheek and Flash Stegman off to keep a lookout, which left no one on tap but Wishbone and his one-eyed foreman.

"Now," Hannah said, "about that matter of compensation . . . ?"

"You knew I was strapped before you took on this job."

"Yeah. But now you've come into your inheritance there's plenty of ways you can rake up some cash. Sell off a few cows or some of them horses. That oughta do for a starter."

"I'm sometimes a little slow in the head," Wishbone said bluntly, "but I catch on fast. If you figured to come out here an' set yourself up as another Hannigan you got another think comin'. I might look to you like a babe in the woods —"

"Not at all, boss," Hannah said in his most unctuous fashion, "not at all. Just wanted to know where I stand is all."

"You stand about ten notches lower than I do. *I* give the orders round here, and any time that don't suit you, you have my permission to hunt another job. Is that clear?"

Hannah's grin disappeared and was replaced by an ugly scowl. "I got a right to know where I stand. I wanta know what you figger on payin' me."

"You get eighty and found for bossin' the crew."

"An' no bonus?"

"Bonus for what?"

"For riddin' this place of Hannigan and his under-strappers."

"As I recollect, it was *you* came to *me* with that prop-osition. If you could pull it off, I said, you'd be fore-man, and foreman you'll be so long as you give satis-faction — just that long and no longer. Savvy?"

There was a murderous look in Hannah's good eye. He swelled up his chest like a pouter pigeon, but before he could do anything there was a gun leaping into Wishbone's hand, its muzzle a scant three feet from his briskit.

Startled, the man took a step back, all his belligerence vanishing. His jaw dropped open. It took him a while to find enough spit to swallow with. At last, getting hold of himself, he said, "Sure thing. You're the boss."

"Make sure you remember it," Reilly growled and, wheeling away, strode into his new home.

Ten minutes went by before he'd calmed himself down and got the adrenalin out of his system. It was plain enough now: this bunch had to go. Left to his own devices, this one-eyed bugger wouldn't wait too long to make a bid to take over. But how could Wishbone keep this from happening? Actually he was in a worse fix than he'd been when Hannigan was ruling the roost. Hannigan's crew had beat him up proper, but with the bunch he had around him now he could be shot and buried before he knew what to watch out for. His survival was dependent on constant vigilance. He couldn't shut his eyes for more than ten seconds or he'd be on his way for a harp and a halo!

He paced the floor trying to think his way out of this. One at a time he could deal with them, maybe even take on a pair of them at once. But unless he could keep them from ganging up they might cook his goose before another night passed.

He took his resolve in both hands and went back into the yard to make a start.

There was no one in sight. Maybe Hannah had decided to get rid of him right now. He felt naked standing out here like a sitting duck. Then Hannah stepped out of the barn, a toadeater look on his face. "What's the first order of business you got in mind, boss?"

Not deceived by this display of servility, Wishbone said, "I want an inventory of all livestock. Get Stegman and get at it."

"Right now?"

"You heard me."

Hannah eyed him a moment. "Hey, Flash," he called,

"we got a job to do. Come on," he said when Stegman appeared in the bunkhouse doorway.

After they rode off Reilly looked a while at the Indian, wondering how far he could trust him, if at all. "How'd you like to work for me at forty a month and found?"

The Navajo looked back at him impassively. "All right."

"You needn't say anything to the rest of them. You stick with me an' I'll take care of you. I'm a man that'll stand by his friends till hell freezes. Savvy? But them that does me dirt had better watch out."

Jim Cheek nodded. "My people like that. Same thing."

"First thing I want you to do is head for town straightaway. There's girl at the Alhambra I want fetched out here. She's got a brown mule at the West End Livery. Put her on it an' see that she gets here. Her name," Reilly said, "is Chacha Ronero. She's goin' to keep house for me. Okay?"

"Hokay," Cheek said and swung into his saddle.

Reilly thought, after the Indian had gone, that bringing the girl here before he got rid of the rest of them might put ideas into Hannah's head. But then that might not be so bad; it would give him an excuse to shoot that bastard. He made up his mind he would do it the first time that bucko stepped out of line.

With this resolve Wishbone felt considerably better, and it occurred to him that with no one else around it would be a first-rate time to bury those corpses. Looking for a good place to hide them he eyed approvingly the compost pile, which was mostly manure dumped from the stalls in the barn.

Shoveling this all to one side he got busy, keeping his ears skinned for sound of the two men Hannah had sent after Hannigan. Inside of an hour he had dug a hole about six by seven. He took the belt and holstered pistol off one of the cadavers, dragged the bodies to the ditch and rolled all four of them into it. Then he shoveled the dirt on top of them, stamping it down till the surface was pretty near hard as the ground surrounding it. What dirt was left over he scattered on top, after which he raked the pile of compost over it.

He took the shell belt and holstered gun into the barn and hung it on a nail just inside the door. Then he mucked the stalls into a wheelbarrow and dumped these droppings on top of the pile. With the flat side of the rake he tidied up the miscellaneous signs of his exertions, wheeled the shovel and rake back into the barn and, after looking around, felt reasonably confident the late and unlamented would likely stay where he'd put them.

In the first flush of day, with the sun not yet peering over the hills, the sound of approaching hoofs brought Wishbone out of the house, his Henry rifle in his hand. Turned out to be Bean Belly and Frosty, the pair Hannah'd sent after Hannigan.

"Well," he said when they pulled up in the yard, "did you catch him?"

"Nope," grunted Bean Belly. "He had too good a horse. We never caught up with him. Seemed like he was heading for town. We follered along for more than twenty miles, never once ketchin' sight of him."

"Where's Hannah?" Frosty asked, squinting his mean little eyes as he searched the yard.

"I put him an' Stegman to countin' the livestock."

"Gawd," Frosty said, "that'll take 'em a week!"

"Prob'ly."

"Where's Cheek?"

"Sent him off on an errand. Soon as you two get a little rest I've got a job for you, too."

"Hell," Frosty said, "I never figured to be no ranch hand."

"Better make yourself scarce then," Wishbone told him. "No one but workers will draw wages around here."

"You ain't figgerin' to pay fer what we already done?"

"Nothin' wrong with your hearin'. What I told Hannah was I wanted them fellers out of here. He guaranteed to get them out. I never bargained to hire a bunch of assassins."

"You better watch your lip," Frosty said, looking ugly.

A pretty ferocious look reshaped Reilly's face, and before Frosty was able to do anything he found himself staring into the muzzle of Reilly's rifle. "Go on," said Reilly soft as silk, "get your ugly mug clean off this ranch before I blow your guts right out the back end. An' don't come back or you'll find yourself buried here!"

Chapter Five

Finding himself the target of Reilly's venomous stare, Bean Belly yelled, "Hey, wait!" jerked his horse around on its hind legs and took out after Frosty.

"Good riddance," Wishbone said to the patient Rachel who'd been standing in the middle of the yard, still saddled, the longest part of the night. Noticed at last, she waggled her ears and pawed her reproach as she stuck out her tongue and lapped whiskery lips as if to remind her master it was high time for grub.

"All right, you old goat," he grumbled affectionately, and led her into the barn where he pulled off the saddle, thrust his rifle into its sheath and forked down some hay. When she continued to eye him without budging he got a measure of oats, dumped it into a nosebag and hung it over her head. "An' don't gobble it whole!" Giving her a slap on the rump, he went back to the house to put something on the stove for himself.

He found the kitchen well stocked and was building up the fire when the sound of hooves drifted in from outside. Hurrying into the office, he took a look out the window to discover with considerable relief it was Jim Cheek coming into the yard with his housekeeper and another Indian.

He went to the porch as they were leaving their saddles. "What's this?" he said, his stare fixed on the second redskin.

"He's Navajo," Cheek said solemnly. "Good man. You trust."

"We'll see about that. What's he called?"

"Horse Ketchum. Good shot. Him Christian."

"Yeah? Looks big enough to hunt bears with a switch."

"Not that big." The newcomer grinned. "Jimmie said you could use some help."

"Yeah," said Wishbone, looking him over. He had a beak of a nose, granite chin and an efficient manner. Long black hair was draped in a pigtail over his shoulder and a folded red rag encircled his head. He had a steady eye. Liking what he saw, Reilly stretched out a hand and found it gripped in a reassuring clasp. "Consider yourself on the payroll," he said, and glanced at Chacha with considerable approval.

"You're just in time to put some grub on the table. Fix enough for all of us."

As the Indians went off to put their horses and the girl's mule in the day pen, Reilly went back in the barn, took the nosebag off Rachel and watched her tackle the hay. He was glad to have Cheek's friend on his side. If he could find one more redskin to put on the payroll, the chances of ridding himself of Hannah and Stegman would be considerably improved. He wouldn't be having to watch his back all the time.

He went into the house to see how Chacha was getting along with their breakfast. The smell of coffee greeted him as he stepped through the door and the delicious aroma of bacon led him to the kitchen, where he found her scrambling eggs in the bacon grease.

He hurried back to the front door. "Come an' git it!" he yelled. Back in the kitchen as he pulled out a chair he said to his housekeeper, "Any trouble with them Injuns?"

She looked around and smiled. "Of course not. Half my father's crew were Indios — the best workers we had. What time will you be wanting lunch?"

"Straight up noon will be somethin' to aim at, but we'll skip it today."

"Good. This place is a pigsty. It will take me the rest of the day to fix it up."

The Indians came in and he waved them to chairs.

After they'd eaten, Jim Cheek took Horse Ketchum on a tour of headquarters, and Wishbone, more to have something to fill up the silence than for any better reason, asked Chacha, "If you were running this spread how would you go about raisin' some cash money?"

"If you've plenty of cattle, you might sell a few head. Or three or four horses maybe. I heard Jim Cheek tell his friend there's some mighty good horses on this ranch."

"There's four in the barn. Let's go take a look at them."

One by one he led them out of the stalls and walked them around to give her a look, knowing from past experience how Mexicans of her class felt about good horseflesh. There wasn't a hacienda in Sonora, or Chihuahua for that matter, that didn't raise their own mounts. Racing, he'd always thought, was bred in the bones of upper-class Mexicans.

She nodded as he put the last horse in its stall. "I'd say by their looks they've got a lot of Traveler or Zantanon blood. Real movers," she said. "If the rest of your horses are anything like these, you shouldn't have much trouble raising cash."

"I'll have Cheek and his friend round up a few," he said, escorting her back to the house. "At the first sign of trouble, you ring that bell in the tower."

He found the Navajos inspecting the corral that was used for a day pen. "This place," said Horse Ketchum, "ain't been kept up too well. These lashes need replacing. Next time you kill a beef we'll make rawhide. All these corrals could stand strengthening."

Nodding, Reilly said, "Right now I want you to round me up about a dozen horses. Put 'em in one of those empty pens. An' keep your eyes peeled for trouble. Hannah an' Stegman are out there someplace. Supposed to be countin' cows."

He saw them off and went back to the house.

Chacha, pausing in her work with a mop, said, "In Mexico most of the larger outfits breed their own horses, keeping one or two good stallions, gelding most of the colts. Always they work to improve the breed. Not often do they send their mares to outside stallions. My father bought his stallions from George Clegg and Ott Adams in Texas."

"Were your horses range bred?"

"Yes. My father believed mares bred in natural conditions produced the best foals and had a higher percentage of pregnancies," she said without blinking an eye. "We had some wonderful horses. Some of the best he raced at the Hipodromo de Las Americas in Mexico City."

"I guess," Wishbone said, "we'll have to use what we've got. Supposed to be a hundred head, so I reckon there'll be a couple of studs anyway. If Hannigan hasn't gotten rid of them. He went outa here like a bat out of hell."

"Perhaps you ought to check what you've got."

"Yeah. Mebbe I ought to," Reilly said grimly and snatched up his hat.

She had the look of wanting to say something else. "Go ahead," Wishbone said, "git it off your chest."

"Well, I was just wondering if you'd had any trouble with those men you brought out here."

"None I couldn't handle. Besides Cheek there's only two of 'em still here. I sent one packin' and another went with him."

He went out to the day pen to pick up his hull, but had second thoughts about making a target out of himself. It'd be a lot more comfortable to do his looking after he'd got Hannah off the place, Wishbone thought, but getting rid of that bucko looked to be about as easy as trimming the whiskers off the man in the moon.

Chapter Six

Looked like there was one thing anyway he'd reason to be thankful for. Seemed pretty obvious Ives Hannah knew nothing about any mine on his property. And he could only hope neither of those rogues stumbled onto it.

Reilly began to wish he hadn't turned them loose on that make-work chore of counting the cattle. At the time he'd wanted to get them out from under foot, but he realized now that letting that pair out of sight might have been a big mistake. If nothing worse came out of it, it had the disadvantage of tying him down here at headquarters.

He blew out a disgusted breath with a curse. For all his supposed self-sufficiency, he was beginning to discover, he had the very bad habit of acting on impulse without looking ahead or pausing to consider where such recklessness might be taking him.

This back-shooting Hannah was apparently a ranny who played all the angles, a man who felt happiest with a good solid edge, but Wishbone shrugged this off, for in his twenty-seven years of knocking around he'd grown used to bucking big odds. When it came down to brass tacks, hadn't he backed the bugger down when the foreman had fetched up that matter of compensation?

He consoled himself with this reassuring thought during the next three weeks while he and his Indians busied themselves with routine tasks. The Navajos brought in a dozen horses, butchered a steer, created a stench with their rawhide-making, strengthened the corrals and ate high on the hog thanks to Chacha's extraordinary skill in the culinary department. She was, Wishbone discovered, a pearl of great price.

Wishbone and Chacha examined the horses fetched to headquarters by Jim Cheek and Horse Ketchum. She pronounced them well superior to the average ranch utility horse, a notion that pleasantly coincided with his own conclusion. Short coupled, with long underlines, wide chests, stout limbs and well set-up quarters, they might not be what are called 'gambler's mounts' but they damn well weren't far from it, he reckoned.

"They ought to fetch a good price in the marketplace," she told him.

"Like what?" he asked.

"Three or four hundred dollars anyway." Looking up at him then, big eyed and with a tremulous smile, she added, "Apiece, I mean."

That was good enough for Wishbone, who had hit on a figure of maybe two hundred.

But as the days passed without any sign of or word from Hannah and Stegman all his previous disquiet began to heat up again. What in the devil were they doing out there? He finally sent Jim Cheek out to look for them, noticing as the Navajo made ready to depart that, instead of packing a rifle as did most of the Indians he'd ever come across, what Cheek had on the saddle under his leg was a scattergun of the sawed-off variety commonly carried by the Wells Fargo express messengers.

On the following day while Wishbone and Horse Ketchum were shoveling down their noon meal they heard approaching hoofbeats and, jumping up in a hurry, Reilly rushed to the office window to behold a strange rider pulling up in the yard.

When he stepped out on the porch the man said, "Howdy. I'm looking for a fellow that calls himself Ives Hannah. Thought perhaps you might have come across him. About your height, heavyset, got a patch over one eye and packs a shooter on each hip." Then he brushed back his vest to show the badge of a deputy U.S. marshal.

"Yeah " Reilly nodded, a clutter of contradictory thoughts fluttering through his head. "Took him on about a month ago as a sort of straw boss. What's he wanted for?"

"The fellow is suspected of having a hand in the robbery of a Tombstone stage carrying mail and a considerable amount of bullion consigned to the bank at Charleston. You got any idea where this jasper's at now?"

"By grab, I haven't. Sent him and another ranny out to get a count on my cows three weeks ago and haven't seen hide nor hair of him since."

"Mind if I look over your holdin' here?"

"Hop to it. Hope you get him. Been considerin' firing the bugger anyway," Reilly said. Then, remembering his manners, he added, "We're just settin' down to grub. Why not come along in an' join us?"

"Well," the lawman said, thoughtfully rubbing his hand along his jaw, "don't mind if I do. Mighty nice of you to share."

So he fetched the marshal into the kitchen, introduced him around and pulled out a chair. "Set an' have a bite, Marshal," he said and told Horse Ketchum to see to the officer's horse. "Been much of that sort of thing goin' on?"

"More than we like. That's the third bullion shipment that's been grabbed in five weeks."

"Was it a Wells Fargo stage?"

"This one was. The other pair jumped Sandy Bob's stage line."

"Anything I can do to help?" inquired Reilly, thinking what a good thing it would be if this fellow should manage to collar Hannah.

"No. I like to play a lone hand. Makes for fewer problems." He accepted a helping of meat from Chacha, then said, "Whatever happened to old Cornelious?"

"Kicked the bucket," Reilly told him. "Fetched me up from Sonora to take over."

After the deputy marshal went off, Wishbone sat on the bunkhouse steps listening to Horse Ketchum recount how it had been in the old days when Ed Schieflin, the man whose discovery had caused the rush resulting in the founding of Tombstone, had still been around. The 'good old days' the pioneers called those times. "Owned the Lucky Cuss," the Navajo said. "About the best silver mine in these parts."

"Say! What do you think of them caballos I've got in the barn?"

"Give a month's pay for any one of them."

Wishbone grinned. "Make it two an' you've got a deal."

The Indian stared. "This bargain day on the Bullybueno?"

"Just a show of faith. I'd do more'n that for a man I could trust. But anyone figures me for a pushover had better watch out. Go ahead. See if any of 'em suit you."

Still staring suspiciously at this crazy Anglo, the Navajo sat awhile as if considering Wishbone's proposition. "I ain't tryin' to buy you," Wishbone declared. "It's just that you an' me hit it off. Hell, I'll *give* you the horse if you can find me another hand competent as you are."

"You're on," said Horse Ketchum. "Let's go have a look."

They went into the barn to examine the horses. The last gelding Reilly led out of its stall was the Indian's choice, a big chunky bay with star and snip and one white stocking.

"When do you want this top hand?" the man asked.

"Sooner the better."

Horse Ketchum nodded. "I'll have him here by morning," he grunted and rode his new horse to the day pen to pick up his saddle.

Chapter Seven

Something Chacha had said about Mexicans and horses had stuck in his mind and given Wishbone a couple of notions that he wanted to put into operation — that is, if Hannah would stay lost long enough and Hannigan didn't fetch in a new crowd of uglies to snatch the place away from him. Unless he could find Cornelious's mine, these ideas he'd been turning over seemed to hold the likeliest and quickest solution to his need for ready cash.

Each morning now for the past three weeks he had climbed from his bunk fully expecting another confrontation with that one-eyed Hannah, and this was beginning to wear on his nerves. He hoped if the deputy failed to find that rascal the threat of his presence here might drive Hannah away. He told Jim Cheek at the breakfast table about the horse he had given Horse Ketchum. "I figure you've got one coming, too. Go pick out one you think would best suit you."

Cheek grunted enigmatically in true Indian fashion and went off to have a look after consuming the entire dish of jelly Chacha had put on the table. Catching her shocked look at the empty dish, Wishbone chuckled. She said, "Won't it make him sick?"

"Nah," Reilly said. "All them Injuns has got cast iron stomachs. They can gobble anything — just like a goat."

Shaking her head, she said, "I've been thinking you might sell some of those horses for match racing. I bet that would be your best market. You might put an ad in the Tombstone papers."

"That's a first-rate notion," Wishbone agreed. "I'll just do that next time someone has to go into town."

"You know, now that you've become a big rancher," she said, "you ought to get yourself some decent clothes. In Mexico the caballeros —"

"You wanta put me in one of them monkey suits?"

"Owning a place like this gives a man some importance. You don't want to go around looking like something the dog dragged in."

"Ain't got no dog."

"You know what I mean. You could get yourself a good sombrero —"

"Don't want no sombrero. Ain't a better hatmaker in the whole Southwest than Gammage, the feller who made this bonnet."

"Well, you could at least get yourself some new clothes."

"I'll think about it," Wishbone said, and got out of the house before she could think up something else for him to do. "Women!" he muttered when he got outside. Just the same, Wishbone had to admit the picture of himself dolled up like a *rico* had a curious appeal to his vanity.

About the middle of the morning Horse Ketchum rode in with another Indian. A tall wiry jasper with straight shoulder-length hair black as a crow's wing, he wore an undented ten-gallon hat with an eagle's feather stuck straight up from the band.

"Name's Rimfire Jones," Horse Ketchum said. "Pretty near half white. Been match-racing horses back in the hills. His mother, Pretty Willow, makes baskets — finest ones you'll ever see. Father's a contractor on the reservation."

"Reckon he'd contract to rid me of Hannah?" Reilly joked, but nobody laughed. "Take him over to the day pen," he said after they'd shaken hands, "and have him pick out a horse."

After they'd gone off, Chacha stuck her head out the door to say, "At the rate you're getting rid of them you soon won't have any left to sell."

"Hoo hoo," he jeered. "No danger. That lawyer feller down at Hermosillo told me there was a hundred head of horses on this place."

Out at the day pen the new man asked, "What's the big idea?" and Horse Ketchum grinned. "Kind of loco in the *cabeza,* like most of these Anglos, but a good man to work for."

Back at the house Reilly found Chacha in the office poring over the ranch ledgers, a perplexed look on her face. "I never saw such a mess," she declared, looking up. "Would you like me to keep these books for you? I used to do it for my father."

"Sure, go ahead," he told her magnanimously, as if it didn't much matter one way or the other. "What's for lunch?"

"I thought we might have some of those steaks before the heat gets at them."

"Good idea," Reilly said, and went off to catch a horse instead of riding Rachel. "If you want to go along," he told the new man, "it'll give you a chance to look over this layout."

So Jones saddled up and they headed north. "Keep your eyes skinned," Wishbone advised. "We got a couple bad eggs roamin' round here someplace. They'd prob'ly just as soon pot us as spit."

Both men had Henry rifles under their left legs. "Hear you been racing horses," Reilly mentioned. "I been thinkin' of putting in a track here. You reckon it would pay?"

"Don't see why not. Never knew an Indian who didn't like a good horse race. Nor a Mexican either. You could charge the owners a small percentage of the purse, put up some bleachers and charge the fans a couple bucks apiece. Once the word gets around, you'd have no trouble fillin' them."

It was sure enough worth thinking about.

Keeping a sharp lookout for Hannah and Stegman, they covered about half the property before Wishbone's stomach reminded him he'd told Chacha Ronero he liked his midday meal at straight-up noon. "Better be gettin' back or we're like to be skinned alive by that girl. Told me she was cookin' steaks for lunch."

On the way back to headquarters they fell in with the deputy marshal who told them, "Nary a sign. Been all over the place twice, an' if that rascal's here he's damn well hid. Reckon he's pulled his freight."

As they rode into the yard Reilly saw a stranger sitting his horse at the edge of the porch talking with Chacha. "Here they come now," he heard the girl say, and the man twisted round to have a look at them. Eyeing the marshal, whose badge was hidden behind his unbuttoned vest, the man said, "Which of you's in charge of this ranch?"

"I am," Wishbone said. "What's botherin' you?"

"Understand from the little lady here you inherited Bullybueno from Cornelious."

"That's right."

"Well, he bought a black studhorse from me about eleven months ago, paying half down and the rest to be paid in six months if the horse proved satisfactory. Not having any word from him I thought I'd better pay him a visit. Didn't know he'd passed on."

"How much did he owe on the horse?" Reilly asked.

"Twenty-three hundred."

Reilly whistled. "I'd like to see some proof of this deal, not that I'm doubtin' your word but . . ."

The stranger dug out his wallet, and after a bit of hunting fished out a paper which he passed over. "Looks like his signature all right," Wishbone said, "but I wasn't a party to this deal and right now I ain't got that kind of money to spend on no horse." He handed back the paper.

The man appeared to be considerably put out. "Then I'll be taking the horse," he said sounding angry.

"Not without more proof than that," Reilly said crustily. And the badge-packer nodded and said, "A wise precaution."

The stranger spun round and scowled. "Who the hell are you to butt in?"

The deputy marshal uncovered his badge. "Ted Bixby." He smiled. "You want to register a complaint?"

"Look," the man said, "I've come a long way, figuring either to get my money or the horse."

"Been smarter to have written before you set out. Mr. Reilly obviously doesn't know you from Adam. Far as we know, you could have got that paper from someone else. Any stranger, knowing Cornelious was dead, could claim he was the man named in that paper. If you've identification, let's have a look at it."

"You ain't heard the last of this," the fellow growled at Reilly. "I'm goin' to see Sheriff Burton!"

"Won't do you no god. I'm outa his jurisdiction," Wishbone said. "If you can't prove you're the gent named in that paper, you better head outa here before I fergit my Christian principles. An' you can tell Hannigan from me I'm not through with him yet."

"Don't know any Hannigan —"

Wishbone beckoned to Jim Cheek. "See this feller off the property."

"By God," the man blustered, "you got a lot of guts treatin' me like some range tramp —"

"Git," Reilly said, and jerked out his pistol.

The fellow's face turned red with rage, but he wheeled his horse and rode off. Cheek followed.

"Reckon you called the turn," Bixby said. "Fellow's an obvious fourflusher or he'd have produced some identification. Who's this fellow Hannigan you mentioned?"

"Found him in charge of this place when I arrived. When I said I was the heir, he had some of his hands beat up on me. When I got patched up, I come back with some help this rascal Hannah recruited and run him off the place."

"Who's for steak and refried beans, hot rolls and jelly and coffee to wash it down with?" Chacha called, poking her head out the door.

"Better sit in an' git your share," Reilly told the deputy; and Bixby said with a grin, "Wouldn't miss it for the world!"

Chapter Eight

As they pushed back their chairs and drank a last cup of coffee, Wishbone said, "South of the border there's quite a bit of match racing. Do we have any laws against such a pastime?"

"Not that I know of," Bixby answered. "Certainly none around here. What's on your mind?"

"I've been turnin' over the notion of maybe putting in a track, a 660-yard straightaway. I've got to rake up some cash money to keep this spread going."

"In some of the states farther east," Bixby said, "I understand they don't permit any form of gambling. The church crowd figure gambling brings in an undesirable element. They've some pretty stiff laws to prevent it."

Chacha said, "They have those laws in Mexico, too, but people like to bet and they have never managed to stop it down there. It has made it rather difficult to get up a match. Usually it takes an awful amount of time and patience and no one can discover the identity of the horses. I don't think you'd really want that here."

Wishbone said, "If I was to go into it I'd want it done openly in an aboveboard fashion. And I'd want to do everything possible to insure fair competition. None of this lap-an'-tap stuff. I'd want to build some kind of a starting gate, have an official starter and another judge at the finish line, and put in a two-lane track that's level as it's possible to make it."

"You could charge the owners of the competing horses a percentage of the purse. Put up bleachers," Bixby said, "and charge the public an admission fee."

"That's it." Wishbone nodded. "Maybe put some ads in the local papers to let folks know what we're up to."

"Apt to take a bit of cash to get it going," the deputy said.

"I could sell off enough cattle to take care of that."

"What you've in mind is strictly a match-race operation, I take it. If you need an official starter I'm your man," Bixby said, "anytime federal duties are not occupying my attention. Cornelious had this whole place fenced, so it's pretty obvious any cattle you've got belong to Bullybueno. You could hold a private roundup and cull your herd, selling off whatever cows an' steers you didn't want to keep."

"Yeah. There's a good level stretch on the way up from our gate that looks flat as a tabletop, which is where I'm thinkin' of putting my straightaway."

"Well," Bixby said, "I've got to be going. Good luck with your project and," he said to Chacha, "*muchas gracias* for this bang-up feed."

The more he pondered the possibilities, the more Reilly was convinced a match-race track was the answer to his most pressing problem: the need to raise money fast. If the track proved financially successful, it would also improve his chance of selling horses at a worthwhile profit. With three willing workers — which he figured to have in these Navajos — it shouldn't cost a heap to put in that track. Higher up there was timber from which he could cut rails and posts sufficient for his purpose. About all he'd actually have to buy would be the mechanism for his starting gate.

Chacha Ronero, with her mop of black hair and tremulous smile, had gone back to the office to work some more on "the mess" the ranch ledgers had become. She came out of there abruptly in a hard-breathing rush to find Wishbone still on the veranda. She said indignantly, "Do you realize what somebody's done to you? They've sold off two hundred steers from this ranch!"

He jumped to his feet. "How do you know?"

"It's right there in the books — sold just a month before you came out here."

"Who done it?"

"No way of telling from the way these books have been kept, but it must have been Hannigan."

"Just let me git my hands on him! I'll rattle the teeth plumb outa his head!"

"That won't do any good, and the worst of it is there's nothing to show what's been done with the money."

"Well," Reilly said, calming down a little, "if it's gone, it's gone. Don't see what I can do about it now."

"You can have him arrested!"

"Not a federal offense, and out of Burton's jurisdiction."

"What's that got to do with anything? He's sold some of your property and pocketed the proceeds!"

"Yes, well I don't know where he's got to," Wishbone said looking sullen.

"If it was me, I'd find out," she snapped, giving him a look most men wouldn't take even if came from their wives. "What's got into you? You must have swapped your backbone for a bunch of fiddle strings!"

Reilly's expression told her she had gone too far. The

breath caught in her throat and she backed off a step, but all Reilly did was get off his perch and head for the bunkhouse without another word.

He was riled all right, riled aplenty, but that feller Hannigan wasn't the kind to be prodded with impunity. Wishbone thought he would sooner tangle with a sore-backed rattler!

Just the same, the thought of that loss and the money that bugger had pocketed continued to gnaw on him until it hurt as bad as an infected tooth. It bothered him all the rest of the day, simmering like a wet wood fire. And the way that danged girl had looked at him piled on more fuel. By ten o'clock that night, unable to sleep, Wishbone strode out of the house, saddled up his mule and headed for town.

In the course of that trip he had ample time for a lot of second thoughts, but none of the dire pictures conjured in this process quite managed to turn him back. It was hardly likely, he told himself, that he would come across Hannigan anyway, and being in town would give him the chance to tell the newspapers about the racetrack he proposed to build.

The sun was well up and it was around nine o'clock when he came jogging into Tombstone. First off he went to have a talk with Harold Burton.

The sheriff said, "I haven't seen Hannigan for a couple of months. I doubt that he's around or I'd have heard of it. If you can use some good advice, stay away from that feller. He's killed three men that I know of."

"Then why ain't he in jail?"

"Because," the sheriff said, "on each occasion the other man drew first with plenty of witnesses upholdin' the fact."

Wishbone mulled this over as he went up Fifth to Allen Street, stopping off at the Oriental to cut the dust from his throat. He tried not to feel too glad about

Hannigan not having been seen around town, but having nerved himself up for a possible confrontation, he supposed he was sort of disappointed in a rather mild way.

Having flushed out his system, he stopped off at the Tombstone *Epitaph* and also at the *Nugget* to tell their editors about the track he wanted to build. "Back East I've heard they used to race horses down the village streets, same thing in the Carolinas, but lap-an'-tap or ask-an'-answer is old hat now. Them hard-boot boys is usin' startin' gates, which take the shenanigans out of the sport — we'll have startin' gates at my track too," he said with a fine show of knowledge.

Back on the street, his head in the clouds, still picturing his track and the crowds it would fetch, Wishbone came near walking straight into one of those big-wheeled, high-sided rumbling ore wagons bound for the mill at Charleston. He jumped back to the curses of the big-hatted skinner striding along at the side of the wagon directing five pairs of husky mules by jerkline, his free hand clenched about the coils of a long black whip that looked thin as a rat's tail.

"Watch where you're goin', Mac!" the skinner shouted. "You git under them wheels, you'll git ironed out flat as a ribbon!"

Reilly glared after him while crossing the street to reclaim Rachel and hit out for home. Had he been dolled up as that dang girl wanted him, he reckoned that feller wouldn't have opened his mouth.

Which got him to thinking about a new suit of duds more befitting his newly elevated position as one of the community's ranch-owning barons. Back in the saddle, still fuming and cussing, he was about to pass the Cochise Hardware and Trading Company's premises when, struck by a thought, he pulled up and went in. The clerk couldn't figure what he was talking about when he asked if they had any starting-gate mechanisms. He tried to explain, but the man stared at him open-mouthed like Wishbone was talking Greek at him.

Disgusted at such ignorance Reilly stomped out and climbed back in his saddle.

Probably have to make a trip to Tucson, he reckoned. And just about then he spotted a sign a few doors down that said B. Laventhal's Clothing. He turned Rachel that way, remembering the day Chacha had said he looked like a range tramp. He went in, peering round, and, with a grimace of disgust, came out again. Two doors below he saw another clothing sign and decided he might as well see what he might find there. The proprietor, wearing a gray derby hat and clenching a half-smoked cigar in his mouth, took him in at a glance and in the friendliest manner said, "Jacob Meyers. At your service. How may I help you?"

"My housekeeper — she's Mexican — says I look like a tramp. What can you do about it?"

"Mexican, you say? Right this way. I've just the thing for you, young sir. Ordered for a gentleman from Mexico City who got shot on the street of this barbarous place before he could get round to picking it up. Happily it's just your size, I believe." He opened up a wardrobe and lifted out a charro costume whose braid caught Wishbone's interest at once. "Here," the proprietor said, "step into this fitting room and try it on. And whom do I have the privilege of serving?"

"Thomas Reilly," Wishbone said with his nose in the air. "I'm the feller that owns Bullybueno," and carrying the suit he went into the little cubicle to find out if he could get into it.

"Ah, Don Tomas!" Jacob cried a few moments later, his face lighting up. "One could hardly believe what these clothes do for you! It's amazing, no less — positively astonishing!"

"You reckon they become me?" asked Wishbone, admiring himself in the full-length mirror.

"Become?" said Meyers. "My friend, the Aga Khan could look no better! One would think they were made for you." Then his face wrinkled up around the dead stogie. "There is just one thing . . . you need the hat that goes with it."

He bustled off and came back with a red sombrero that had tiny silver bells hanging from the great rolled brim. This he set on Wishbone's head and stepped back to observe him, beaming with satisfaction. "Behold — a *rico* absolutely."

"I'll take the whole works," Wishbone said. "How much?"

Jacob Meyers assumed a pensive expression. Presently he said, "For you, my friend, one hundred dollars."

Wishbone's jaw sort of dropped a bit lower, but he jerked it up so fast it could hardly be noticed. "Charge it to Bullybueno," he said grandly; and Jacob Meyer, re-kindling his stogie, nodded. "Of course. Of course. We will open an account."

Hauling open the drawer of a nearby display table, he fetched out a pad of forms, headed the top one with the ranch's name, filled in the price and made a little X near the bottom. "If you'll be so kind, just sign right there, Don Tomas."

"Yeah — better pick me out a couple shirts to go with it."

While the proprietor was doing so and wrapping them neatly, Reilly, inside the cubicle, was divesting himself of the new apparel and slipping into his old dusty duds. The proprietor called, "I throw in the shirts, Don Tomas, to our better acquaintance."

"Thanks a lot," Wishbone said, and picked up the suit, shirts and sombrero in their tissue-lined cardboard boxes with JACOB MEYERS lettered in curlicues on the outside. Then he went out to his mule, tied the boxes to the saddle strings, got aboard and turned Rachel toward home. As Wishbone rode out of town he noticed a great shaggy dog trotting discretely along about a rope's length behind.

Chapter Nine

Coming into the yard at Bullybueno, Reilly espied a strange horse ground-hitched alongside the porch and a strange jasper in town clothes standing at the bottom step jawing at Chacha, who stood in the open door. While Reilly stopped to stare, the big dog, who had followed him the whole distance, loped up to pause beside him, looking up at him as if waiting for orders.

"There he is," Chacha told the stranger and went back inside.

The man swung round. "You the feller that heired this spread?"

"What about it?"

"Your name Thomas Reilly?"

"Look," Wishbone said, his patience wearing thin, "whatever you're sellin' we don't want any."

"Ha ha. Very funny," the man said, showing no inclination to laugh. "I've got in my hand three hundred an' forty dollars' worth of your paper. IOUs if you want to be precise. What do you figure to do about it?"

"I never so much as laid eyes on you before —"

"That's neither here nor there. You comin' up with the money? Because, if not, I'll put a lien on this place an —"

"Git!" Reilly said, and the dog came off his haunches with a wolfish growl. The fellow took one look, dived for his horse and piled into the saddle — minus the seat of his pants which was in the shaggy dog's jaws. The man jerked out a nickel-plated revolver and looked about to squeeze off a shot when Reilly's silk-soft voice said, "You shoot that dog an' I'll bury you here."

They glared at each other for about ten seconds. Then the fellow, half strangled with rage, declared, "I'll have you in court before the week is out! I'll — "

"Go get him," Reilly said, and the big shaggy dog took off with the man's hard-running horse barely two jumps ahead of him.

Reilly, carrying both boxes, went into the house. "Where's them Injuns?"

"Out gathering the cows you said you wanted to sell."

Wishbone, grunting, took the boxes into his room and shut the door. When he came out ten minutes later Chacha eyed him up and down. "Well?" he asked.

"You should have got some new boots while you were at it. I thought you were broke."

"Got this outfit on tick," Wishbone said. "Do you like it?"

"You look so grand now — except for the boots and that mare's nest of hair — we'll have to call you Don Tomas."

"Yeah," Wishbone said, "that's what that clothin' feller called me. Don Tomas. Got a real flashy sound, don't you think?"

"Where'd you find that mutt? Not planning to keep him, are you?"

"Hell, he adopted me. Follered me all the way out from town. Course I'll keep him. Poor little stray."

"He may be a stray, but he's certainly not little," she said with a sniff.

"You see the way he run off that collector? Took the seat right out of his pants! He knows what to do an' does it — no arguin'. Be good company for you when I ain't around." He shook his head to hear the bells tinkle.

She was considering him critically with no sign of the deference she'd originally accorded him. "You've no more idea of the fitting and proper — of how to conduct yourself as a *ranchero* — than a twelve-year-old boy. Which is what you remind me of!"

"Oh, I do, do I?" Wishbone stuck out his lip. "I guess you've fergot you was a stray, too, 'fore I took you in! Now it's do this an' don't do that every time I turn round! You're a good one to yap about the fittin' an' proper — who the hell heired this place anyhow?" And he stamped out of the house like the boy she had called him.

Jim Cheek was the only Indian who came in for supper. If he noted the new *rico* get-up on Reilly or the red sombrero with the tinkling bells the boss wore to the table, he didn't mention it. He reported they had 150 head of prime steers rounded up for the sale and asked for instructions on what was to be done with them. Chacha half opened her mouth, then abruptly shut it when Wishbone glared at her and said, "You can put them in those two holdin' pens and I'll write out a ad you can put in them Tombstone newspapers. No use drivin' them cows to town if we can get a buyer to come out here after 'em."

Soon as they'd eaten he followed the Navajo out. "You put a brand on them critters?"

It seemed the ones they had chosen were already branded; not, he guessed, that it made much difference if he could persuade any buyers to come out here after them. "Tell you what," he said. "I'll write out four ads, an' you can come back by way of Tucson an' put the extra two in the papers there. Did you see my new dog layin' back of the stove? Follered me all the way back from town."

"Might come handy," the Indian said. "Has good eye."

"Yeah. That's what I'm callin' him. Good Eye."

Next morning the Navajos drove in the steers; and, giving Cheek the ads he'd written for the newspapers, Wishbone sent him off to town with them. The other two hands he took to the place he planned to use as the site of his match-race track, about midway between the gate and the house. After that he took them up into the hills to his timber crop and got them started cutting the requisite number of rails and posts. "We're puttin' rails on each side and a rail down the center so there'll not be any bumping, or one of 'em cuttin' the other one off," he explained.

Back at headquarters he found a fringe-topped surrey standing in the yard behind two matched bays. The owner was still aboard and keeping a sharp eye on the large shaggy dog staring back at him from the veranda right in front of the door.

Wishbone pulled up a few feet away. "You lookin' for me?"

"If you're the heir to Bullybueno I am."

"So what's on your mind?"

"Came out to see if you'd sell this place."

"Not interested in sellin'."

"I'm acting for a group that would like to take it over."

"The answer's still no. Don't waste no more breath. Just turn that rig around an' head back to where you come from. Pronto."

The man looked from Reilly to the dog and back.

Then he got his surrey turned around and drove off muttering under his breath.

"Yes sir, Good Eye, I reckon you're just what we need around here," Wishbone told the dog.

It had occurred to him while trying to get to sleep the night before that somehow, somewhere, he was over-looking something, or maybe forgetting something he ought to be remembering. But try as he would he could not remember it; it seemed to hang there just out of reach. And he'd a feeling — an uneasy feeling — it was something important.

And about an hour later it came over him what it was. Since he'd got dolled up in these charro duds he'd been waltzing around with no gun on his hip. "No wonder I been nervous," he muttered, and hurried into the house to strap his shell belt around himself. Feeling a bit more confident, he went outside and propped a hip against the veranda rail to contemplate the view old Cornelious had bequeathed to him.

After a few minutes he got to thinking about the mine the Hermosillo lawyer had mentioned. You'd have ex-pected if there was one, somebody would have stumbled onto it by this time, he thought. Chunks of silver big as a washtub, that feller had said.

Gad, if he could locate that mine, his position in the community would assume an importance no one could deny!

It was certainly something to think about.

Good Eye came over and lay down at Wishbone's feet, resting his jowls on outstretched paws, the very picture of contentment.

Chapter Ten

Wishbone Reilly was seldom tactful and there were certainly several other things a diligent person would have no trouble pointing out that he wasn't, but no one could say he was not observant. He guessed he had put Chacha's nose out of joint. She hadn't said one word to him since he'd got out of bed. So here he was, sitting around like a bump on a log with no one to talk to except maybe Good Eye, who seldom engaged in needless chit-chat. When Good Eye spoke he commanded attention.

If Cornelious had had a mine on this place, it was either just a pocket or damn well hidden. Maybe it was up there where the boys were cutting rails and posts, he thought. Be easier to hide a mine in the woods, screening the entrance with brush or something.

The dog had already learned his new name; smart as a whip. When he stood upright he was tall as a bear. Streetwise and manwise, he looked to Reilly like a real asset. Could be a big help in smiting these Philistines that appeared to be beating a path to his door. Hell, he'd proved that already!

Rimfire Jones rode in to report they were running out of young stuff suitable for cutting into rails up there. "How about them hills about a mile east of our gate?" Reilly asked.

Jones looked surprised. "You own them?"

"What difference does that make? Ain't nobody usin' them."

"Fine," said the half Navajo. "We'll go over there first thing tomorrow."

"Might's well stay for grub now you're here."

So Jones took his noon feed off Chacha's cooking, cleaned up his plate till you could see your face in it. He even thanked the girl and said it was a heap better than he was used to.

After he rode off, Wishbone went out and sat on the steps awhile still pawing over the things on his mind. Considering what Bixby, that deputy, had said, he decided Hannah and Stegman must have lit out for greener pastures, which wasn't no loss. The really dangerous one though was that dang Hannigan.

He'd had a good thing here and it was unlikely that Bullybueno had heard the last of him. Wishbone thought he wouldn't be surprised if Hannah went and teamed up with him. And that, by grab, would be outside of enough!

In fact, he would not be surprised if that ranny who had tried to sell him back those IOUs hadn't been set on him by Hannigan. Right in the midst of these reflections he spied a buggy coming up the lane from the gate, and it sure enough looked like a female was handling the reins. "Keep your seat," he told Good Eye, "till I see what she wants. Prob'ly lost her way an' wants directions."

He came down off the steps when she swung into the yard and pulled up about ten feet from the porch. Wishbone could tell right off she had all the right attributes in all the right places. He hair, which she wore piled up on her head, was as yellow as a field of ripe wheat;

her lips were red as strawberries; and her eyes were cornflower blue. In fact, she had about the loveliest face he'd ever put his peepers on — *stunning* was the word that jumped into his mind.

"Who are you?" she demanded, examining him with those blue eyes and looking suddenly colder than a bartender's heart.

Her words jerked Wishbone out of his trance, and with an elegant flourish he swept off his sombrero and bowed in the manner of a Spanish grandee. "I am Don Tomas of the Hacienda Bullybueno, entirely at your service, ma'am."

"Yeah? You putting me on? Where the hell is that lying rat Cornelious?"

The contrast between her looks and speech should have put him on guard, but Wishbone was too carried away by this gorgeous creature's delectable exterior to notice the hard look in her eyes.

"I expect you mean my uncle. The sad truth of the matter is that he passed away several months ago —"

"Passed away where?"

"That ain't exactly known. But he's gone. Kicked the bucket — cashed in his chips, took a runnin' jump across the Divide."

"You mean to say the old fart's *dead*?"

That should have jogged him, but Wishbone, chained to her chariot in a manner of speaking, only bobbed his head. "I'm afraid so," he said. "You knew him well?"

"You can bet your last nickel on that! But not so well as I thought, it seems. Took me in proper with them fancy promises! Which is all I ever got out of . . . Oh, a few trinkets maybe, but what he said was —"

"Well, I'm sorry about that but," Reilly said, beginning to wake up, "what the man said cuts no ice with me. I expect Cornelious said a lot of things besides his prayers, an' none of 'em's bindin' on me. You get the picture?"

"You're turning me away?" she asked in disbelief.

"Hard lines, miss, but that's what it boils down to. Bullybueno's mine an' I ain't takin' in boarders."

She threw a despairing glance about and Reilly, following it, discovered the sun was scarcely half an half from dropping behind those western crags.

"I drove about sixty miles from the stage line at Tombstone getting to this godforsaken place an' now you expect me to turn round and drive back? That sweet-talking sonofabitch promised this would be my home . . ."

"Yes, well, you got to look at the facts. Cornelious is dead and buried an' I ain't fixed to take in guests."

She looked about to dissolve in tears. "What am I to *do*? It's been a most exhausting trip — I doubt I've the strength to face such a drive in the dark." She began to sound desperate and peered at him in the most imploring way. "Couldn't you at least put me up for the night?" she cried.

Compassion overcame him, and against his better judgment he found himself saying, "Well, just for the night."

At which point Chacha appeared on the porch. "What's going on out here?" she asked.

"This lady's come out here on the mistaken notion the place still belonged to Cornelious. Like you know we ain't fixed to put up guests —"

"I suppose if it's just for the night we could manage."

"That's what I've told her," Wishbone said, a bit dubious now. And the blonde said, "I'm Miss Farradine, Cornelious's promised bride — Gresselda Farradine, the actress. You know — *Blowing Bubbles*, been running two years to packed houses in Mexico City. It's awfully good of you to put me up. When do we eat? My stomach thinks I've gone off and left it."

By the time Wishbone got through packing in her luggage, his stomach felt like it had left him, too. And he was beginning to believe he'd made a horrible mistake. There was no proof but her word that Cornelious had ever laid eyes on her. That "promised bride" had stuck in his craw. Maybe the old goat had fallen for her and made a fool of himself, but . . . Smothering an oath, he drove around to the day pen and put up her horses.

By the time he got back to the house, grub was on the table and Miss Farradine was wading into it like a pack rat chewing up the last of the bedding. "I've eaten better," she said, "but this ain't half bad." She waved a fork in his direction. "Better draw up a chair."

He had just sat down when the sound of hooves was heard. A few minutes later the three Navajos filed in and Chacha went back to the stove to cook up more vittles.

Reilly waved them to chairs. "An unexpected guest from Mexico City. This here's my crew, Jim Cheek, Horse Ketchum an' Rimfire Jones." He passed around what was left on the platters. "Be more comin' up directly," he grunted.

Chacha came in with a skillet of refried beans and some sowbelly, which she divided among the boss and his hands. A few minutes later she hustled back in with a plate of hot rolls and a jug of sorghum, which she set down with a thump.

Next morning, after the hands had been fed and gone off, Wishbone and Chacha sat over their coffee for a considerable spell, both of them waiting for the unwelcome guest to put in an appearance. Chacha finally cleared off the table and, back in the kitchen, began to wash up the dishes, making enough noise to wake up the dead.

It was close to eleven when Miss Farradine appeared. A robe wrapped around her, she languidly asked, "What's for breakfast, honey?"

"Breakfast," Reilly said, "was over five hours ago. Your team's in the yard all ready to go."

"It's too late to start now. I must have overslept."

"Late or not, you're startin' in ten minutes. Better wriggle into some clothes." He looked at her grimly. "Unless you're plannin' to give the jackrabbits a treat."

"I couldn't possibly leave now. Be dark before I —"

"Dark or not, you're leavin' pronto if I have to carry you out along with your luggage."

She glared at him then and Reilly glared back. He called, "Good Eye! Come in here!"

Chacha gasped, "Don't set that dog on her!"

The sight of that monstrous black shape in the doorway made Miss Farridine forget all else. She scrambled for her room like the heel flies were after her and slammed the door with a vicious thud. Winking at Chacha, Wishbone said, loud enough to make sure Cornelious's promised bride heard him, "Dog, go fetch them Injuns."

And then to the female in the next room he said, "You got eight minutes left to be on your way. An' if you ain't, I'm sendin' them Injuns in after you!"

She came out in a rush, not stopping to dress, one battered suitcase in each hand, and dashed through the side door in a run for the buggy.

Chapter Eleven

When the boys rode in from their rail- and post-cutting job, Rimfire Jones looked around and asked, "Where's Little Bo Peep?"

"If you mean that yeller-haired wench," Wishbone said with a scowl, "I sent her packin'."

Rimfire, looking like a kid deprived of his teddy bear, said, "Dang if you ain't an old killjoy, boss. Ain't you got no brotherly feelin'? I was figurin' to talk her into sharin' my hogan."

Horse Ketchum laughed. "With that face an' all, I bet she figured to be here through Christmas. Claimed to be your uncle's promised squaw the way I heard it."

"Never got out of bed till eleven this morning," Cha-cha said disdainfully as she put a platter of steaks on the table.

"About as comfortable to be around as a dose of poison ivy," Reilly declared, shooting a covert look at his housekeeper.

"I coulda tamed her," Rimfire drawled. "Just the kind I

like. Soft an' cuddly with just the right touch of temper. Like chili in a Spanish omelet."

"Eat your steaks before they get cold!" Chacha snapped, flouncing back to the stove.

The Navajos looked at each other and grinned.

Wishbone smiled slightly, but muttered under his breath, "*Cuidado, hombres.* Our pussycat's got sharp claws." In a normal voice he said, "How you comin' along with that wood cuttin'? Think you'll have it wrapped up time the week's out?"

Jim Cheek said, "Tomorrow maybe."

"Better snake them rails from the east-side hills before somebody catches you cuttin' up there."

"You tryin' to teach grandma how to suck eggs?" Horse asked.

"Just tryin' to keep outa trouble," Wishbone said. "Expect we better butcher another steer or maybe even two to make enough rawhide strings for them posts."

"Two ought to do it," Horse Ketchum declared.

"Who's diggin' the post holes?" Rimfire asked.

"Now you've mentioned it, guess you're elected," Reilly told him.

"You tryin' to cripple me for life?"

"Wouldn't want to cripple your gun arm anyway. If it looks like bein' too much, I'll git you some help."

After they'd put Chacha's vittles away and stepped outside, Reilly said to Cheek, "Better keep that shotgun handy."

"You got a feelin'?"

"I got a hunch we been about as long with quiet as we're like to get," Wishbone said and stared broodingly at the distant hills. "Somethin's goin' to happen pretty quick."

"If it's Hannigan on your mind," Rimfire said, "he's pretty foxy. Might be waitin' till this track's set up."

"You know him?" Wishbone asked, narrowing his eyes.

"Can't say I ever met him, but I've heard a few things off an' on about that jigger. Got a bad reputation."

Reilly felt a cold shiver coursing up his back as he followed the Indians out to the saddling pen. It was like someone was dancing across his grave, he thought as he saddled Rachel.

He went back to the house and got his rifle, wondering edgily if wearing these fancy duds might be kind of like tempting fate. Then his natural optimism took over. After losing four hands the last time they'd clashed, it didn't seem like that rogue would stick his neck out this soon.

Thinking about the Bullybueno horses, he realized that, if he could organize a breed association like the Thoroughbreds had in the Jockey Club, it might help in selling off some of his extra bangtails and in furnishing sprinters for his track. He could call it the Range Horse Breeders of America. He liked the sound of that and decided he could get out some certificates or registration papers, done in fancy inks to stir up enthusiasm. Might be he'd got hold of something, Wishbone thought excitedly. But it wouldn't help much on a local basis; that was two-bit stuff. What it needed was a national outlook. Same as the Jockey Club. Hell, he could headquarter it right here at Bullybueno! This was a damn good notion, he told himself, offering him plenty of possibilities.

So, riding along thinking up ways and means, he got a little careless about keeping his eyes skinned as he came into the hills. First thing he knew, something tugged at his sombrero — a good hard cuff that might have taken it off his head if it hadn't been chin-strapped.

This was almost instantly followed by the crack of a rifle, and Wishbone woke up to the real world around him like a startled rabbit. Slamming his spurs into Rachel and ducking low along her neck, he urged her on toward a hackberry thicket on the nearest slope.

Pulling up back of this thin protection, rifle in hands, he looked around frantically without seeing any movement or telltale drift of smoke. No one had to tell him he'd been mighty lucky!

He stayed where he was for another ten minutes, still fiercely watching to catch some sight of the sniper, but without avail. The villain must have made off while his target was scrambling for shelter. Reilly had no doubt but that the would-be assassin would come back for another chance. It was a bushwhacker habit.

He hurried on to find where his men had been cutting. When he got there he was happy to find it wasn't noticeable to the casual eye. You'd have to look pretty close. The boys were doing a first-rate job. Presently he heard the sounds of their efforts and came to where a pair of them were wielding the saw.

"Thought I heard a shot," Rimfire said and then just stared at Wishbone. "Take a look at that overgrowed hat you're wearin'."

Wishbone, snatching it off, glowered at the two holes puncturing its crown.

" 'Bout a inch lower un' we'd be luggin' you off to the happy huntin' ground, Reilly."

"Yeah," Wishbone growled, putting his hat on again. "One of them shoot-an'-run polecats."

Rimfire said, "You better quit travelin' solo for a while. Damn good way to get yourself killed." And, "If this keeps up we oughta be drawin' fightin' pay."

"Maybe we better leave the rest of this awhile," Reilly said, "an' snake down the stuff you've got already cut. We can count 'em then and see where we're at."

So they began hunting out the cut rails and throwing them into a pile. Reilly took down his rope and shook out a loop into which they thrust the ends of about twenty poles. Wishbone tightened the noose, got back in the saddle and headed for the flats. "Goin' to leave plenty sign," Horse Ketchum said, looking after him.

Jim Cheek shook his head, and Rimfire said, "Sometimes he don't give a damn about nothin'."

"You fellers take off with the rest of these rails," Horse Ketchum said, "and I'll smooth out the tracks." He spoke a few words in the Navajo tongue and it sounded to Wishbone a heap like a turkey gobbling.

Reilly dragged his load to where the track was to be, got down, loosened the loop and threw it off, then coiled up his rope and hung it back on the saddle. Jim Cheek and Rimfire dragged up their loads and Wishbone began laying out a line of them to the decided-on distance. "We better use a chalk line before settin' the posts," he told them. "Six feet from this one you can lay out another."

"What about them rails we left up in our hills?" Rimfire asked. "Bunch of posts up there, too."

"Where's Horse Ketchum?"

"Tidyin' up; he'll be along pretty quick — Hey! there he comes now."

When Horse joined them, Wishbone sent all three of them after the stuff from the original cut and went on laying out rails in the second row, six feet from the first and parallel to it. What he had on hand soon ran out with only one batch extending the full 660 yards. His start on the second had got but a third of the way when he ran out of rails. Sure was going to take a pile of poles, he told himself, eyeing his handiwork. And dang near twice as many posts. But there'd be nothing like it this side of the Rockies, and once it was up and everything was whitewashed, it ought to bring sightseers from miles around.

Be a good idea to get them Range Horse Breeders of America certificates printed up to have on hand for the grand opening, Reilly thought. For who could say they wouldn't go like hotcakes? And, at ten dollars each, he'd have real money coming in. That thought sparked the idea to limit the match races to only those horses certified by the association.

Still thinking about the pros and cons of this, he climbed onto Rachel and headed for home, looking off in the gathering dusk for the first sign of Good Eye and wondering if Chacha had yet started supper.

He'd only half a mile to go so he was letting Rachel pick her own pace. She was a free-striding critter with a long reach of leg but wasn't minded to hustle when left to her own devices.

Wishbone had just turned into the yard and was about to swing down when some sixth sense stopped him; he clung there motionless, both eyes probing the darker patches of shadow that hung about the buildings.

And then he saw it, something that seemed to stick out from the darkest corner of the bunkhouse. He stepped off the mule about twelve feet from the water trough, the sixteen-shot Henry rigid in his fist. He didn't take his eyes off that projection for one second. It seemed to be getting bigger and blacker and taller as he watched, and all of a sudden he knew it was a man. Without waiting any longer he squeezed off a shot. The black shape yelled and spun away from the wall. Then it staggered and went down.

Reilly dived for the water trough with blue whistlers whining past him and rifles banging from two directions. He started to poke his head around the end of the trough and something hit him a hell of a clout. A million stars seemed to burst in his brain. Then he felt himself slipping down a long spiral into a place where no light had ever been.

Chapter Twelve

Drawn by the dread sound of rifles, Chacha Ronero flung herself through the door just in time to see Reilly fall. Without thinking of her own peril, she rushed to the water trough and the wounded heir to Bullybueno.

At the sight of the blood, an agonized look contorted her face, and she sank beside him pulling off his sombrero and cradling that pitiful head in her lap. Her heart hammering, she heard and saw nothing of the racket and yells that went on around her until Rimfire Jones, squatting beside her, growled, "He ain't dead yet! Just let me get at him!"

He snatched a flask from his pocket and emptied it over the bloody wound. Reilly yelped and came bolt upright off her lap. With the blood washed away, the half Navajo snorted while Reilly swore and stared wildly around him. "Wrap somethin' around it — he'll be all right," Rimfire said, getting onto his feet. "He's got more lives than a goddamn cat!" Then he went off to turn over the shape at the bunkhouse corner, scratching a match to have a clear look at him. By this time the girl had Wishbone up with a rag round his head and she was holding him with both hands.

Cheek, piling off his horse with Horse Ketchum behind him, said disgustedly, "Got clean away — the both of them."

"What you got there?" Ketchum demanded.

Rimfire said, "Looks like Flash Stegman, a sidekick of Hannah's. I'm bettin' Ives Hannah was one of that pair you let get away."

Wishbone moaned, then managed to ask, "What the hell happened to me?"

Rimfire said, "Reckon you'll have to settle for a headache. All you got was a crease across that bony knob you use for a head."

Next morning Reilly felt close enough to normal, except for a sore head, to go out with his crew and supervise work at the site of his straightaway. He sent Jim Cheek off to town for a wagonload of two-by-twelve planks from which Reilly hoped to construct his starting gate. Horse Ketchum and Jones fetched the rest of the rails down out of the hills.

By the time they knocked off for supper they had three lines of rails six feet apart laid out for a distance of 660 yards. "After that wagon gits here with the planks and carriage bolts," Wishbone said, "we'll use it to bring down them posts."

Next morning at breakfast Wishbone told his crew about his plans for organizing the Range Horse Breeders of America. Though they looked a bit dubious, none of them offered any serious objections, and Reilly then disclosed his idea of allowing no horses to compete on his straightaway except those owned by members of his new association.

This was greeted with considerable skepticism. Chacha declared, "I don't believe they'll go for it. Unless you can sign up most of the roundabout ranchers, you'll not get enough match races to pay for the work and expense you put into it."

"Hoo hoo," Reilly jeered. "You just watch! No matter what, if somethin' good comes along everyone an' his uncle will want to be in on it. That's plain human nature. I'll make this deal look so good there won't none of 'em feel they can afford to be left out. I'll have signs up in every post office in Arizona an' every general store in Chihuahua and Sonora. You'll see!"

"I guess," Rimfire said, "there'll be plenty fools who'll join your association, but they'll balk like bay steers at puttin' up more *dinero* to compete on your track."

"Some of 'em might," Wishbone agreed, "but if they've got any faith in the ability of their horses, they'll not let a few more bucks keep 'em out! Most of these ranchers are gamblers at heart or they wouldn't be ranchers in the first place, an' damn near everybody likes to see a good horse race. We got a good thing here an' I'm goin' to plug it for all it's worth."

Chacha nodded, and Horse Ketchum said earnestly, "I believe you. If we can just get it started it ought to roll like an avalanche."

Jim Cheek returned with the wagonload of planks for the starting gate, and Wishbone talked the driver into taking the wagon up to where they'd been sawing and fetching back a load of posts. "I want to get them posts down here," he said, "an' you can put your time onto the bill for them planks. I'm not expectin' you to do this for nothing. If it takes that long, I'll even throw in your supper."

By the time the first load of posts came down Rimfire had dug twenty-five of the holes to set them in, a task Reilly started him on straightaway. They'd staked twine along the course to make sure the lanes were straight, so Rimfire had no trouble knowing where to put his holes.

When the second load of posts came down from the hills Reilly took Jim off that detail to lend Jones a hand with the digging. This speeded up the work remarkably, with each of them trying to outdo the other. When the wagon showed up with the third and last load of posts it was getting so late Reilly called it a day and they all set out to put a meal under their belts.

Good Eye lay on the ranch-house porch, his eyes half closed, but his tail started thumping as soon as he saw Reilly among the approaching group.

"That's a lot of dog you got there," the man from the lumberyard said, looking nervous.

"You bet," Reilly said. "An' he can pick out friend from foe at first glance."

"Just to be on the safe side, you tell him I'm a friend."

Wishbone laughed. "He knows. Don't you, Good Eye?" and the shaggy tail thumped some more on the porch.

"You're just in time," Chacha said from the door and tossed Good Eye a bone. "I'm dishing up now."

When the man started back for town in his wagon, Wishbone rode alongside on Rachel. For it was time, he reckoned, to get his posters advertising the track printed up and into the mails, and to put ads about the breeders association into the Tombstone papers. He figured the stringers for out-of-town papers would take care of getting the news around.

They got into town about ten the next morning, and Reilly's first stop was at the office of the Tombstone *Epitaph*, where he placed a full-page ad which described both the Range Horse Breeders association and the straightaway track being built for match racing. He also mentioned the ruling that only horses owned by members would be eligible to compete. Anyone who had ten dollars could become a member, whether he planned to race or not. Then he decided to include that the track would charge a fee of fifteen percent of the purse put up for each race in advance of the running.

"And when do you plan to pay for the ad?" the *Epitaph's* editor asked.

"Soon as I get some money coming in."

"That's pretty indefinite isn't it?"

"Well, there's nothin' indefinite about me owning Bullybueno — you can check with the sheriff. If that don't satisfy you, you can come out to the ranch and pick you out a fat steer. That should take care of it."

"For a good fat steer I'll give you two full pages. How about me giving you the first page next week and the second the last of the month?"

"I want to hit 'em hard right off the bat. One this week an' one next."

"Make it next week for the first page and two weeks later for the second full page, and I'll throw in a full page in the *Prospector* in between?"

"Done!" Wishbone said, and shook his hand enthusiastically.

Then he rode on down to the jail for another confab with Sheriff Harold Burton. "You said," he reminded the sheriff, "that Bullybueno was out of your jurisdiction." At the sheriff's confirming nod, he asked, "All right, I'm out of the town marshal's bailiwick, too. An' except for federal problems I'm not going to be bothered by the U.S. marshal's office — right?"

"That's essentially so," Burton admitted.

"So, actually, I've got no protection at all from the law around here?"

"I'm afraid that's about the size of it," the sheriff admitted. "If you hold match races out there, you'll have to police them yourself."

"So what I want is the name of a good trustworthy gunslinger and where to git hold of him."

Burton took a good long look at Wishbone but finally

nodded. "Try Jack Flack. When he's not working he can usually be found at Billy King's saloon."

Wishbone got back on his mule and headed for Billy King's. At the saloon he told King what he wanted, and the saloonkeeper pointed toward a man sitting at a table near the back wall.

Flack looked to be in his middle twenties, a lean, sharp-featured, dark-skinned man who had an overgrown straw-colored mustache and wore a dark brown shirt, a mule-skinner's hat and old blue jeans stuffed into knee-length Hyer boots. He had the coldest stare Reilly had ever looked into.

"My name's Reilly," Wishbone told him, "heir to Bullybueno. I'm in possession as of right now, havin' run Hannigan out of there. I don't think I've seen the last of him, and some bushwhackin' varmint is takin' considerable interest in my health. Burton tells me you can be trusted. What'll it take to put you on the payroll?"

While Wishbone spoke, Flack gave him a pretty keen scrutiny. "Hundred a month," the gunslinger said. "A full month's pay whether I'm there a month or no more than a day."

"I'm short on cash. Your choice of a steer or cow every month for as long as you're out there?"

Flack thought it over for a few seconds then nodded. "You got yourself a deal. When do I start?"

"As of right now. Meet you at the West End Corral in about half an hour."

Feeling a heap more comfortable, Wishbone rode over to the office of Charles M. Smith, Commission Merchant, and inquired about the chances of selling 100 head of steers. "Man you want to see is Lem Chaney," he was told. "He's a cattle buyer. Got himself an office at Nellie Cashman's American Hotel on Fremont between Fourth an' Fifth."

So Wishbone got himself over there and found Chaney on tap. "Sure," the cattle buyer said, "I'll take delivery on your ranch at twelve cents a pound and be out there tomorrow with enough hands to move 'em."

Wishbone's next stop was at the grocery establishment of Fitzhenry and Mansfield's, where he asked if they had such a thing as dog food. "You bet. What size dog you got in mind?"

"Big one — bout the size of a brand-new calf."

"Comes in fifty-pound sacks."

"Don't deliver, do you?"

"Whereabouts?"

"Bullybueno."

" 'Fraid not. Cost you an extry ten bucks if we have to take it way out there."

"Just hang it over the back of my mule. I'll want to open an account with you. Sheriff Burton can tell you I'm the owner; inherited the spread from Cornelious."

"Be glad to have you for a customer," Mansfield said, shaking hands.

Going west on Fremont, on his way to pick up Flack, Reilly happened to be looking down Fourth as he passed and caught a fleeting glimpse of two men and a blonde woman going into Hafford's Corner Saloon.

Brief though his look at them had been, it was enough to give him a pretty good jolt, for the woman was unmistakably that bitchy Farradine actress, and one of the pair of men with her was just as surely Ives Hannah. As if that wasn't bad enough, the other one looked sure as hell like Hannigan!

Chapter Thirteen

Sight of those three together provoked in Reilly more than a few discomforting thoughts. Nobody had to tell Wishbone all three had it in for him; any kid could have figured that out in two shakes. In the past three or four days it had crossed his mind more than once that Hannigan might well have been back of that visit by his uncle's "promised bride." What really gave him cause for concern, though, was the apparent proof that Hannah had teamed up with Hannigan.

It had been this possibility that had led him to hire Jack Flack. But now he wondered if Flack would be enough.

He might have to hire a whole army of gunslingers to keep Bullybueno out of Hannigan's grasp. For it was plain enough now that Hannigan had no intention of leaving matters as they stood.

He found Flack waiting at the West End Corral, and as they started for the ranch he gave the gunslinger a terse rundown of the things that had happened since he'd come into his inheritance, winding up with seeing those three going into Hafford's saloon.

Flack nodded. "Up to more skulduggery, I reckon."

"Look," Wishbone growled, "I hired you to keep them wolves off my back!"

"Don't worry," Flack said without the least hint of concern.

Wishbone swallowed uncomfortably, not at all reassured. "That Hannigan's pure poison!"

"The man's a fool," Flack said, sneering. "If he comes nosin' round I'll take care of him."

That was fine, as far as it went, Wishbone thought, but in his view it might not go far enough. Bushwhackers were a pretty cheap commodity around Tombstone, which bragged of having a man for breakfast 365 days of the year. But drawing a shuddery breath, he kept his mouth shut. He didn't want his gunfighter thinking him scared.

"What kind of dog have you got out there?" Flack asked, eyeing the sack draped over the back of Reilly's saddle.

"Big black shaggy dog. Smart as a whip! Don't do much talkin' but he sizes folks up in nothin' flat."

"Knows up from down, does he?"

"You bet."

After that they didn't have much to say to each other. They camped that night in a thicket of pretty fair-sized umbrella trees alongside a pool of green-scummed water, and they dined off jerky strips from Reilly's saddlebags.

They reached Bullybueno a little after nine the next morning and paused at the track site while Reilly looked over the work in progress. Rimfire came up to say, "We're still short of posts. Horse Ketchum discovered a slope in them eastern hills that he figures will give us enough to finish that last lane."

"This ought to do fine. I've got some news I'll hand out when we put on the nosebags. Meanwhile let me make you acquainted with the newest recruit to the Bullybueno crew — Jack Flack. Jack, shake hands with Rimfire Jones, one of our most valuable possessions."

"Aw, shucks," Jones muttered, gripping the gunfighter's mitt, "you got to discount a heap the boss tells you. He's in the habit of spreading things on with a trowel." Turning to Reilly he said, "Them planks are here for the startin' gate."

"Yeah," Wishbone said, "I noticed. Big problem now is findin' some way to make 'em open an' shut."

"All we need is a couple big springs, a few bolts an' some iron."

Flack said, "I believe the Arizona Iron Works off Fremont Street should have most of what you'll need, mebbe all of it. What they ain't got, they can fix right quick."

Wishbone said, "You want to take care of that, Rimfire?"

"Sure, I'll ride in after supper. You want I should get enough powder to mix up some whitewash? Take about twenty gallons, I figure."

Wishbone nodded.

"If it sets right with you, I'll stay here for a spell," Flack announced. "I'd say this track's about as vulnerable to vandals as anything you've got."

"I been thinkin' as much myself," Rimfire said.

Just as Wishbone was about to head for the house, Lem Chaney, the cattle buyer, showed up with two cowhands, so Reilly went off with them to help round up the hundred head of steers Chaney had agreed to buy.

The ranch was supposed, according to the Hermosillo lawyer, to have uncounted cattle, which Reilly had assumed to be a great many. But riding over his range in the hottest part of the day, they didn't scare up as many as he'd expected. Of course that bastard Hannigan had sold off 200 head, but that shouldn't have left him this short. According to Chacha, who'd been keeping the books, that sale of 200 was all she'd come across. So where were the rest?

"A good many of them, I expect," said the buyer, "will be down in the breaks hunting shade."

"Damn!" Wishbone said, much put out. "What's wrong with my head? I got a hundred an' fifty penned steers at the ranch. Boys brought them in last week — don't know what I been thinkin' of."

"Guess you got a lot on your mind. What you need's a secretary, Reilly," the cattle buyer said. "I know a girl . . . matter of fact, she's my wife's neice . . . "

But Wishbone was already heading for home. Another female underfoot was one complication he wanted no part of!

The boys who'd gone to that wooded slope Rimfire had found had snaked down another batch of posts, and Rimfire and Flack had already set them while Reilly had been off with the cattle-buying contingent. He guessed another thirty posts would about do it. That reminded him of the raw and buried hides still to be cut up.

He mentioned this to Horse Ketchum, who said he'd get at it soon as they had those last thirty posts. "What about the uprights an' planks for them bleachers?" Reilly asked.

Jim Cheek said he'd ordered them, and Rimfire said he'd check with the lumberyard when he went after the stuff for the starting gate and whitewash. Wishbone remarked it would probably take at least two wagons, and maybe three, to fetch all the lumber he'd need for the seats he wanted built as well as the siding for the back. He also thought they'd better have a couple five gallon drums of green paint for the gates. "I don't want no half-ass job," he told Rimfire.

Then he herded the cattle buyer and the two cowhands up to headquarters for a look at the steers in the two holding pens. After a critical inspection, Chaney announced himself satisfied and, allowing he'd take the whole shooting match, he whipped out his checkbook and paid then and there.

Chapter Fourteen

"Whoow-ee!" Reilly gasped after that bunch of steers had been led away and the last of the posts had been set and tamped into position. "Let's go eat!"

Having cared for their mounts and cleaned themselves up a mite at the water bucket outside the back door, Reilly and his crew shuffled into the kitchen. Just as they were sitting down round the table, Chacha, wielding a broom, chased Good Eye through the house and out the front door.

"I'm not going to have that dratted dog in the house!" she informed Reilly, her eyes blazing. "How you expect me to cook and get meals on the table with that great hulk underfoot, watching every move I make and sitting there drooling like a leaky faucet!"

When Wishbone, evading her scorching glance, kept his mouth tightly shut, she declared "I'm not going to have it, do you hear?"

Reilly gathered up what was left of his dignity and, putting the best face he could on the matter, introduced the latest member of their team. "And that's another thing!" she told him angrily. "I want to see you in the front office soon's you've finished wolfing down that grub!"

With chastened looks they all dug in. It was not long before the last platter emptied and the poker-faced crew was shuffling out the back door and heading for the bunkhouse.

Reilly, attempting to get in the first strike, growled, "When I put you on the payroll I wasn't figurin' to be hirin' no loud-mouthed shrew —"

"Shrew, is it?" Chacha snapped, giving him a torrid look. "When I was *invited* to come out here and keep your house I was distinctly told that I would not have to cook for the hands, that aside from keeping the place tidy and getting your meals I was to be my own boss! If I had known I'd be no better than a peon, I'd have stayed where I was!"

Wishbone threw up his hands. "All right, so I forgot about that. I've had enough on my plate without fightin' with you. I'll try to git me a dough wrangler — one of them all-around chuckwagon kind — an' take that much of it off your shoulders." He then said, meek as a church mouse, "I did invite you to come out here an' sure didn't mean for you to be no slave. I can only say that, what with one thing an' another, I been too taken up to notice the amount of work I been heapin' on you. If you can find it possible to put up with me, I'll raise your pay another twenty bucks."

"It's not the money," she said blushing as intensely as she had when he'd first propositioned her. "It's . . . it's . . ." She turned away, but not before he'd seen the big tears welling up in her eyes.

Reilly shook his head, completely bewildered. You'd expect a twenty-dollar raise and hiring a cook for the hands would have fetched a bright smile, he thought. He heaved a great sigh and went out on the veranda to slump down beside Good Eye.

Which was where Rimfire found him when he rode up ready to head for town. "Well," the half Navajo said, grinning cheerfully, "reckon I better be on my way."

"Hope you can remember all the things you're supposed to fetch. That lime-an'-chalk powder for the whitewash, the stuff for the startin' gate, the lumber an' green paint for the bleachers an' them other things I told you about. An' you better fetch back a cook for the hands. Chacha thinks I'm pilin' too much on her."

After Rimfire left, Wishbone sat awhile longer trying to figure out what was really wrong with Chacha. He couldn't see what she had to complain about with a good home and all. Good Eye, plainly commiserating with him, licked his ear, which reminded him the dog hadn't yet been fed. Sighing, he said "Come on" and headed for the barn with Good Eye at his heels.

It wasn't until later, when he was trying to get to sleep, that Wishbone abruptly remembered he'd forgotten to give Rimfire the cattle buyer's check to bank. Maybe, he thought, it was just as well. Though he hated to make another trip to town, it would be better to open the account himself. He needed a checkbook and some ready cash, and probably he'd better pay for that lumber. Not only that, he'd sure as hell need a supply of canned goods and staples for the bunkhouse cook he'd told Rimfire to fetch.

Another thing he'd forgotten to mention at supper was seeing the Farradine woman going into Hafford's Corner Saloon with Ives Hannah and Hannigan. If there were any hard feelings between them, it had not been apparent.

Reilly now felt pretty sure that the night he'd been jumped out there by the water trough that Stegman's companions just about had to be Hannigan and Hannah.

He reckoned that while he was in Tombstone it might be a good idea to get something for Chacha, something personal that might help bring back whatever it was that had caught his fancy when he'd offered her the job all those weeks ago.

Bright and early he fed the dog and instructed the hands in what he wanted taken care of during the day. Then Wishbone set off for town on one of the day pen horses. He reckoned it might be dark before he got there, but by adopting the cavalry system of alternately walking and trotting he hoped to arrive before Hudson and Company's bank shut its door.

He'd not been long on his way and was in his third trot when he spied a cloud of dust ahead of him. Resting the sixteen-shot Henry rifle across his lap and with both eyes skinned, he braced himself for trouble. But the dust turned out to have been kicked up by Rimfire and a slight pigtailed fellow in a black skullcap whom the half Navajo introduced as Lum Fung, the new Bullybueno cook he had hired.

"He speak any English?"

"Sure — spik good," the man answered for himself. "Long time cook fancy restlant."

"What I had in mind," Wishbone said, "was a chuck-wagon cook."

"Cook chucklagon, too — cook anything," Lum Fung declared, grinning earnestly.

"Lumber'll be here tomorrow," Rimfire assured him, "an' I've got the stuff right here for the whitewash an' startin' gate."

"Good. Get 'em started with that whitewash right away."

It wasn't much past five-thirty when Reilly rode into Tombstone and found the bank still open. With the cattle buyer's check, he opened an account for Bullybueno, drew out a couple hundred dollars and got himself a checkbook with which he presented himself at the lumber company's office. Introducing himself, he said he'd come in to pay for three wagonloads of lumber supposed to be on its way to Bullybueno.

"You'll have it out there tomorrow," the clerk told him, accepting the check and receipting his bill.

With this chore taken care of he went back to Fifth Street, left his mount at the tie rail and entered a store. "I want the best machine you've got in stock, with all the gadgets, and I'll pay for it right now," he said to the proprietor. "It's to go to Miz Earnestina Ronero at Bullybueno, and I'll expect the fellow that delivers it to give her a demonstration and to make sure she knows how to use all them gadgets — savvy?"

"It'll be out there tomorrow," the man promised, putting Wishbone's check in his pocket.

As chance would have it Reilly ran into Bixby as he headed for his horse. "How you doing?" the deputy U.S. marshal asked, shaking hands. "Making any progress with that track?"

"We're aimin' to have the grand opening in about three weeks. The *Epitaph* an' the *Prospector* will keep the public informed. You had any luck runnin' down that feller Hannah?"

"That villain's been keeping a mighty low profile —" Bixby began when Reilly cut rudely into this talk to inform him that no less than three days ago he'd seen Hannah with his own eyes, right here in town. "Saw him an' that damn Hanningan goin' into Hafford's Corner Saloon three days ago."

"You did?" Bixby asked with considerable surprise.

"You bet I did!"

"Much obliged for the tip."

"I'll even give you some help," Wishbone declared whipping out his checkbook. He wrote out a check and passed it to Bixby. "Here's a hundred bucks. Put up a reward an' let's get some action. That bugger's made two attempts on my life — see this scar?" he demanded, yanking off his sombrero. "He tries again I might not be so lucky!"

Still fuming and fretting, he headed for home. It was a pretty dark night with no moon showing, and before he had gone ten miles he began to have a disquieting notion that someone was dogging his tracks. He tried several shifts but failed to see or hear anything. Even when he stopped to put an ear to the ground he could hear no sound of hoofs.

But the belief he was being followed would not go away. He pulled off the trail and hid, but though he waited for more than ten minutes he did not see or hear anything. Muttering under his breath, his rifle slippery in his sweaty hands, he pushed on, frequently throwing nervous looks behind him.

There were plenty of stars, and out in the desert it was a lot less dark than it had been farther back, but try as he would Wishbone still couldn't locate anyone following him. He got down twice more to put an ear to the ground, but on neither occasion could he detect any sound. Whoever was back there was certainly no amateur at this kind of thing.

With his nerves rubbed raw, Reilly pulled up once again in a thicket of mesquite, determined to wait, rifle ready, for the stalker to show. He stood there beside his horse for a good half hour and finally, swearing, took off at a lope, not by any means satisfied he had the night to himself. The worst of it was, he thought nervously, the fellow may have cut around him and might be waiting up ahead someplace, waiting for the quarry to blunder into his sights.

Chapter Fifteen

Despite all Wishbone's worrying, nothing untoward happened and he arrived intact at Bullybueno next morning shortly before noon to find the posts and rails of his straightaway track glistening white in the sun.

Rimfire was laying out the planks for the starting gate while Horse Ketchum and Jim Cheek heckled him mercilessly. Meanwhile, the poker-faced Flack was teaching Good Eye to shake hands. Wishbone said nothing about the ghost rider he'd never caught sight of. Rimfire announced, "I've got two pairs of doors for this thing when it's built. They're coming from the carpenter shop sometime tomorrow."

"Tomorrow, tomorrow," Wishbone muttered. "Everything's mañana around this place!"

"Well," Rimfire said, "I've got Hill's solemn word they'll be here tomorrow or we get them at half price."

"I hope to hell they'll fit," Reilly growled, and rode around trying to decide the best place to put the bleachers. Between the track and the house, he presently concluded, and came back to ask Rimfire, "When you planted Steg-man, what did you do with his iron an' his rifle?"

"Hung his shell belt just inside the barn where that other one was hangin' and stood the rifle against the wall right under them." At that moment Horse Ketchum said, "There comes the lumber for them bleachers," and Reilly, following his look, saw three wagons, each of them hauled by two teams of horses, slowly working their way down the last hill. "Did you think to order siding?" he asked the half Navajo, and Rimfire nodded.

"Everything's in hand," he replied.

Then Reilly asked, "Anybody think to take a look in that mail box?"

Jim Cheek said he'd looked, but it was empty as a woodbox during a heat wave.

"What's the next thing on the agenda?" Flack asked.

"Gettin' them bleachers up," Wishbone said, "an' I want the whole crew workin' on them long as you can see to drive a nail." He pointed north of the track. "Off there is where I want 'em, about sixty feet back."

"I bought carriage bolts," Rimfire said, "to anchor them uprights."

"Where's that damn Chink?" Wishbone asked.

"Up at the bunkhouse gettin' settled in. Lookin' over them pots an' pans," Cheek said. "When are his supplies due?"

"They told me we should have them by nightfall," Reilly answered and rode off to tell the wagon drivers where he wanted the lumber and other material un-loaded.

He came back then and took Rimfire aside as the other members of his crew helped unload the wagons. "Did you get the springs and the other things you wanted for those gates?"

"Sure thing," Rimfire said. "They're putting some of the stuff on at the carpenter shop. The rest I'll put on when they get here; when it's time for the horses to bust out of the gates, all the starter'll have to do is push a little lever."

"An' both gates will open at once?"

"Absolutely. You ever been on a horsecar or trolley? Same kinda thing opens their doors."

"Well," Reilly said, "I just hope it works."

"It'll work." The half Navajo appeared supremely confident. "I got a flair for that kinda thing." He swung around abruptly. "There comes your stuff for the bunkhouse cook."

By the time it got too dark to drive a nail and the crew was ready to put on the nosebags, they had the studding for the bleachers already up and some of the crosspieces anchored in place.

At the house, Wishbone sat all by himself at the kitchen table. Without giving any thought to how it might sound, he said, "Now the crew's outa here you might's well be takin' your meals with me."

Standing by the stove, Chacha Ronero said tartly, "Where I come from the kitchen help would not so much as even dare *think* of sitting down with the *patrón*."

"You've left all that; you're in the land of the free. Up here everybody's equal," said Wishbone testily, "an' if it pleases me to eat with my housekeeper, she better set another place and sit down there pronto." He saw her look down demurely then.

In a humble tone, but with no sign of pleasure and making no effort to hustle, she murmured, "Yes, Don Tomas," and set another plate and another cup and saucer. Soon she added black bone-handled eating utensils. When she observed her slowness was making him scowl, she got the skillet off the stove and put a small portion of its contents on her plate.

"And get yourself some coffee an' get your butt into that chair," the *patrón* ordered, "before I lose my temper."

"*Si, Señor.*"

"An' quit actin' like a goddamn slave!" Reilly snarled, fiercely eyeing her expressionless face. "What the hell's got into you, woman?"

She picked up her fork and pushed the food around her plate without putting any of it into her mouth. Exasperated, Wishbone yanked the napkin from the neck of his shirt, jumped up and stomped from the room.

At their next meal she had nothing to say beyond a murmured, "*Buenas dias, Señor*," and avoided his glance until Wishbone, feeling like the king of fools, gulped down his food and, with Good Eye at his heels, hurried down to the track. Work appeared to be progressing well, with about a third of the plank seats already bolted in place. His spirits lifting, he discovered that the doors for the starting gates were being fitted into place by the meticulous Rimfire. As usual, Horse Ketchum was being free with his comments and advice.

About midmorning the present he'd bought for Chacha arrived on a pack mule and was sent on up to the house straightaway together with the ginghams and calicoes and odd lengths of cloth that had been included for the demonstration.

Reilly was lending a hand with the work on the bleachers when a radiant Chacha ran from the house to fling her arms around his neck and kiss him vigorously on both cheeks, oblivious to the staring crew. "*Una máquina!*" she cried. "Oh, thank you, Tomas, for the wonderful gift. I have never been so delighted!"

Embarrassed, feeling the heat climbing into his face, Wishbone struggled out of her embrace and with what dignity he could muster muttered, "*Por nada*, Chacha." Despite his actions, he felt inordinately pleased by the smiles she lavished on him and was glad to be back in her good graces again. Wishbone had begun to worry that the gift might have offended the temperamental Mexican. Still smiling, as excited as a child on Christmas morn, she hurried back to the house to try out the *máquina de coser* for herself.

He shook his head, for it was only a sewing machine after all.

He scowled at the grinning hands. "Back to your work, hombres — *andale, pronto!*"

"Hey!" Flack said, pointing. "That ranny put somethin' into your RFD box."

"I'll get it," Cheek said, and went off toward the distant gate to come back with a rolled up newspaper. "I wonder . . ." Wishbone said, on seeing he held a copy of the Tombstone *Epitaph*. Hastily opening it, he found on the back of the front page the big ad he'd promised a cow for. "How's that?" he said, proudly handing it to Flack as the others crowded round.

"Cripes! Lookit the front page," Rimfire exclaimed, and there, spread over half of it, was the complete story of Reilly inheriting Bullybueno and telling of the first-rate track he'd built for match races, plus a full paragraph about the Range Horse Breeders of America.

"Guess that'll put us on the map," Horse Ketchum said.

"Say — look here," cried Rimfire suddenly. "There's a reward of one hundred bucks 'for information leading to the arrest and conviction of Ives Hannah, wanted for robbery of the U.S. Mail!'"

"How about that?" Wishbone said, looking smug. And Rimfire, reading on, said, "'Anyone having information as to the whereabouts of Hannah is asked to get in touch with the U.S. Marshal's Office at Tombstone.' An' there's a full description of the bugger."

"I hope they catch him," Wishbone muttered. "Does it say he's dangerous?"

"Yep — 'armed and dangerous,' " Horse Ketchum said.

"Let's git to work on them bleachers," Reilly grumbled. "Standin' round gabbin' won't butter no parsnips."

"Wait a sec," Flack said, staring gateward. "Company comin'."

Chapter Sixteen

Reilly spun around like a startled fawn. But it wasn't Hannah or Hannigan, just some galoot in range clothes coming up the lane on a bald-faced bay.

"Runnin' horse man," Jim Cheek informed them. "Name's Ashford. Got a piebald geldin' he calls Giddy Joe."

Wishbone, pricking up his ears, got the scowl off his face and replaced it with a welcoming smile. "Howdy, Ashford. What can we do you for?" he said as the man pulled up before them.

"I come out here to apply for membership in that Range Horse outfit. You the feller that heired this place?"

"That's me, Tom Reilly," Wishbone said, reaching up to shake his hand. "You raisin' horses?"

"A few," Ashford said. "That make me eligible?"

"You bet. Come up to the house an' I'll fix you up. Understand you're a runnin' horse man."

"Got one I run when I can find any takers. That's one

reason I was glad to learn about your association and track. Bring in some outside horses, maybe."

"We sure hope so," Reilly admitted as he got out an application form. "This here's for fellers that plan to match race. You fill out one of these for each of the bangtails you figure on racing."

Ashford said, "One'll be enough for me. How much?"

"Ten bucks. Be sure you fill in the markings of your horse."

As Ashford filled out the form, Wishbone, looking over his shoulder, said, "Giddy Joe, eh? Seems like I've heard that name before. Tell you what: if you can fix up a match in the next couple weeks, we'll schedule it for our grand opening. Be three weeks from yesterday."

"My horse ain't used to startin' gates, Reilly."

"You're welcome to give him all the practice you want. The big advantage of starting gates is it takes all the shenanigans out of gettin' them off. The lap-an'-tap method could sometimes take up to an hour, each of the riders tryin' for the edge. This way, when them gates open, both horses have an equal chance."

Ashford didn't seem too happy with that remark. "Another thing," Wishbone said, "on a two-lane track with a divider between you won't git bumped or lose any ground by being forced over one way or another. Each horse runs in his own lane an' stays there."

He couldn't tell if Ashford liked that or not. Some of these old-time brush-track jaspers counted on such maneuverings to bring them first to the finish, Wishbone thought. With the heavier horse they would force the competition into taking extra steps.

"What happens if your horse gets hung up in the gate?"

"He'll git beat, I reckon."

"On a six-sixty-yard race, what happens when the horse gets to the end of it? He go plowin' through the crowd?"

"No. We got one more rail to add to this track; purpose of that is to hold the crowd back. Any gent caught on the wrong side will be fined or barred from any future meets — or both," Wishbone told him. "With this kind of operation there'll be no skulduggery."

Ashford, whatever he might be thinking, offered no comment.

About half an hour after Ashford left, Reilly got to thinking about his empty mailbox, recollecting there never had been one piece of mail in it. When he mentioned this oddity to Horse Ketchum, the Navajo said, "Too far out. If you've got any mail, they're probably holdin' it in town. General Delivery, maybe. You want I should go in an' find out?"

"No. I'll send Jimmy. I want you and the rest to get out about thirty more rails and enough posts to anchor 'em. I wanta run the crowd-side rail out another forty yards or so. Maybe you better git right at it."

So Jim Cheek was sent off to town to pick up any Bullybueno mail the post office might be holding. The other two Navajos set out for the hills with their cross-cut saw.

Three days later they'd snaked in enough rails and posts to give horses running 660 yards some protection from an exuberant crowd. But a new worry was festering in Reilly's mind. Jim Cheek hadn't yet showed up with the mail he'd been sent to find out about. "Reckon Cheek's quit?" he asked Rimfire.

Rimfire shook his head. "Wouldn't think it like him to take off without collectin' his pay."

When another day passed with no word from Cheek, the boss of Bullybueno, anxious to find out if that *Epitaph* ad was pulling any mail, set off after supper to see for himself. He'd always figured Jim Cheek for a man who had no use for liquor, but firewater was the curse of a good many redskins. Who was to say Jim wasn't off on a bender?

Around nine the next morning Reilly rode into town. Dodging a couple of mule-drawn ore wagons, he made straight for the post office at the corner of Fourth and Fremont and asked if there was any mail for Thomas Reilly or Bullybueno. The postmaster gave him a sour look and said, "I've been holdin' a heap of mail for you. You'd do well to invest in a big P.O. box or have your correspondents address you in care of General Delivery."

"I'll take a box," Wishbone said, then paid for the box and filled out the form.

"What you need," the man said, "is a sack. Hold on an' I'll see if I can find you one."

He came back after a bit carrying a battered old tow sack bulging with mail. "Mostly horse registry stuff it looks like."

The sack on his shoulder, Reilly had just stepped out of the office when the sheriff came hurrying up to say, "Just the feller I'm lookin' for. You got a Injun named Jim Cheek on your payroll?"

"Sure. What about him?"

"Well, he's dead," Burton said matter-of-factly. "Found back of Rafferty's saloon with three slugs in his back."

Wishbone looked considerably upset. "When was this?"

"Yesterday morning. He's over at Ratter's Undertakin' Parlor, Allen Street just beyond Sixth. You got any idea who might have polished him off?"

"Only one I can think of is that one-eyed Hannah feller. Cheek used to work for him."

After riding over to Ritter's, Wishbone viewed the body, told the undertaker to bury him in Boot Hill and handed over the price. "He was a damn good Injun," Reilly said as he was leaving.

Wasting no further time, he got on his mule and headed for home, the tow sack lashed behind his saddle and his Henry rifle held across his lap. Though he studied his backtrail frequently and with a good deal of care, he could find no sign of being followed this trip. If any attempt was being hatched to dispose of him, he reckoned the time of greatest danger would be after the sun went down. He was not ruling out a daylight attempt, but bushwhackers generally preferred to get in their licks after nightfall.

He kept his eyes skinned, munched on some jerky and made sure his rifle was fully loaded. He had no intention of being caught off guard.

The shadows lengthened. Thickets grew darker as dusk closed in around him. With increased vigilance he scanned every likely place for an ambush. If fate decreed he should get shot, he meant to take the assassin with him. He'd been lucky with Stegman, but luck was a mighty thin reed to lean on.

The stars only vaguely lightened the night's deceitful murk, but when the moon came over the distant hills he could see a little better. Though it added to the mileage, he rode well clear of any shadowy places wherever possible.

Not until he saw the lights of Bullybueno did he draw a comfortable breath. Yet even then he kept his eyes skinned, remembering the night he'd been attacked beside the water trough.

Flack's voice cut through the dark as he came into the splotches of lamplight that crisscrossed the yard. "Hold your fire. It's only me," Reilly answered, and pulled Rachel up alongside the steps to the veranda as Good Eye came charging out of the bunkhouse shadows. When he swung down, the dog jumped up, put his paws on Wishbone's shoulders and eagerly licked his face.

Chapter Seventeen

When Wishbone and Chacha sorted through his sack of mail next morning they found fifty-three applications from persons anxious to become members of the new Range Horse Breeders association. The checks and currency enclosed added up to $530. They grinned at each other delightedly. "Looks like we're in business," Reilly said. "Send each of these people blanks when you get time, an' mark 'em paid. Next time somebody goes to town they can take 'em in and mail 'em."

He rode down to have a look at the track and saw the sunlight glinting off the new whitewashed extension the boys had added to hold back the crowd at the finish. This had been Ashford's suggestion, and he thought it a good one. "There's somethin' about that jasper I don't quite cotton to," Flack remarked. "Can't put my finger on what it is," he said, "but somethin' tells me that feller's as crooked as a jackrabbit's hind leg."

"Never knew a match-race hombre yet that wasn't lookin' for a edge if he could find one," Rimfire said, "an' I been round quite a passel of 'em." Then he peered at Reilly like he'd something on his mind and said with some abruptness, "You've got a lot of dang fine horseflesh on this place, Tom. Why don't you let me take two or three of the best in hand and see what I can do with them?"

"You mean leg 'em up for competition?"

"Sure. Why not?"

"If we should come up with a winner, someone's sure to figure the track is rigged."

"Losers are bound to find an excuse whether it makes any sense or not," Horse Ketchum said. "I wouldn't let that stop me. If we should happen to win, it would sure improve the market for our horses."

"That's right," Rimfire said. "Best advertisin' in the world, accordin' to my notion. Everybody wants a winner."

"An' if we lose, what about the market?"

"We'll be no worse off. If we even come close, it's bound to fetch in some buyers who figure to know more about it than we do," Flack said, and the others nodded.

The night before, Wishbone had told them about what had happened to Jim Cheek. He had sometimes wondered how devoted to his interests these Indians were, but their remarks last night had set his mind at rest on that score. He'd also considered hiring another hand or two, but with such supporters as Rimfire and Horse Ketchum and with Jack Flack as a watchdog — not to mention Good Eye — he decided to leave matters as they were for the present.

Rimfire said, "One of those horses in the day pen looks like a pretty good prospect, and if you say the word, I'll get in a couple more off the range."

"Go ahead," Wishbone said. Then, beckoning Flack, he walked over to the rows of seats they'd built just north of the track. With the siding in place, there was space behind and under the seats sufficient to make a couple of good-sized rooms. Pointing, Reilly said, "Tell Rimfire I want both ends of this sealed, and each end's to be fitted with a door and padlock. Make a good place to store stuff."

"Why not have Horse Ketchum do it? Seems to me more important to see what Rimmy can do with them horses."

"Yeah," Wishbone agreed after thinking it over.

After supper that evening Chacha remarked, "You know, I've been thinking. Jim Cheek was one of Hannah's men. Don't you think perhaps he may have been killed because Hannah was afraid of what Cheek might tell you?"

"Jim never told me nothin'," Wishbone said, looking puzzled. "Can't think what he'd know that would advantage me any. More likely he was killed because he'd swapped sides. Still enjoyin' your *máquina?*"

"Oh, yes!" she cried, and looking into her flashing brown eyes Reilly thought that if she'd stayed in town she'd have had to fight suitors off with a club. He was glad she was here, that she was his. Like Bullybueno.

"I have those papers all fixed," she said, "ready for you to mail. You should sign those checks and have them taken to the bank."

"You're right. In fact I'll take them myself," he said and mentioned the box he had rented at the post office. "There might be another pile of mail waiting for me."

"Take that sack for good luck," she urged, putting it into his hands. He gave her a grin, patted her shoulder and went off in high spirits.

In town he bought stamps and stuck them on his letters, which he then poked through the slot in the wall. Next he opened his box and counted the mail in his sack. There were 109 letters, all addressed to the Range Horse Breeders of America.

Back on the street, quite a number of persons nodded

or waved at him while he was securing the sack behind his saddle and several came up to shake his hand and wish him well. Most of them were men he didn't know and couldn't remember ever having seen before. Recognizing his newfound importance, he cocked his red sombrero with its tiny tinkling bells to a rakish slant and thrust out his chest with a good deal of satisfaction

He didn't look much like the down-on-his-luck prospector who had come to Bullybueno scarcely four months before to be set upon and beaten insensible by Hannigan's men.

Stepping into the saddle, he turned down Fourth toward Allen Street, then recalling the checks he'd aimed to deposit, he cut back past the post office and rode up to Hudson and Company's bank.

With the tow sack filled with his newest batch of mail, he went inside to be greeted by a smiling Mr. Hudson, who asked how Wishbone's match-race track was shaping up and what the bank might do for such a valued customer.

Reilly held up his sack. "I got a pile of mail here I have to sort out."

"Come right this way," said the banker, indicating his private office and placing his elegant swivel chair and desk at this public benefactor's disposal. "Make yourself right at home. That track of yours should fetch a heap of money into this town."

Reilly nodded. "Yes," he said, slitting open his envelopes. "I expect it will. Got me a pile of checks an' cash right here I want to deposit."

Sorting the checks into one pile and the cash into another, he put the envelopes and correspondence back into his tow sack and began endorsing the checks, adding the ones he'd received in the first batch to the pile.

"I'll take care of those for you and fetch you a receipt.

Here — try one of these while you're waiting," Mr. Hudson said, holding out a box of imported cigars. "They come from Honduras."

With his deposit slip carefully tucked in his wallet and the tow sack under his arm, Reilly left the bank puffing on the cigar. Then, still feeling his importance, he rode around to Smith and Dyar's stationery store and purchased two long boxes of envelopes, which he took to the commercial printing shop. There he had the Range Horse Breeders of America printed on the back flaps together with his address.

He tried to think if he'd forgotten anything he had aimed to attend to, and it occurred to him Chacha ought to have some means of protection. He bought her a little pearl-handled lady's gun along with cartridges for it. This done, he pointed Rachel toward home.

He was passing the alley alongside the Atlantic Restaurant when he heard something whip past him to wham itself into the corner of the building with the buzz of an angry rattler. He swung round, gun in hand, and saw a knife protruding from the wall. The alley was empty. There was nothing to shoot at. Considerably riled he quit town at a lope.

Chapter Eighteen

Back once more at Bullybueno he found Rimfire school-
ing a three-year-old filly at the starting gates. Flack was
at the lever and Horse Ketchum was giving another filly
some work on the track.

Pulling up at the house, he fetched in the tow sack
and the two boxes of Range Horse envelopes, which he
took into the office and presented to Chacha. He handed
her the pearl-handled derringer and showed her how to
load it. "Don't try to hit anything not close enough to
spit on; but if you do have occasion to use it, all you got
to do is point it and pull the trigger.

"In that sack you'll find opened letters from a hundred
an' nine persons wantin' to join our association," he
announced proudly. "I banked the money. Do the same
thing for these folks you did for the last batch. Mark the
applications *paid* an' . . . Hell, you know more about
what to do than I do."

He rubbed Rachel down and turned her into the day
pen then took himself back to the track without having

mentioned the knife he'd had thrown at him. No use getting Chacha in an uproar. Much as he liked to have her around, like most of her sex he'd ever swapped words with, she was hard to understand sometimes.

As he approached the structure they had built for the prospective match-race fans, Jack Flack turned up to tell him both ends had been sealed off as ordered, and the doors had been fitted. "We found two of these old-time latches on them Dutch doors to the stalls so we put them on, not havin' no extry padlocks around. That all right?"

"They'll do for now," Wishbone said, "but it wasn't to keep things in that I wanted the padlocks, it was to keep people out. How's Rimfire comin' along with them race prospects?"

"Right smart, looks like to me. Been workin' 'em out of them gates two at a time — him an' Horse."

"I take it them doors are workin' okay?"

"Like a charm. If you want to step over to the track, I'll show you."

The half Navajo and the full-blooded one, each on a horse, were just loping back from the end of the track when Reilly and Flack approached the starting gates.

"Mornin', Boss," Rimfire said. "This pair's comin' along pretty good, but it's that filly I brought in from the hills that's goin' to show them what speed's all about. I been workin' her — all of 'em for that matter — in cowboy plates. Put racin' shoes on her, she'll just about fly."

"What do you call this pair?" asked Wishbone.

"Well, that buckskin there is Susie Q. I call this flax-maned sorrel colt Jaime. That okay?"

"I don't care what you call 'em so long's they'll run."

"Third one's a bay three-year-old filly that Chacha thinks we oughta call Whistling Cat. A fast learner, that one. Comes outa them gates like hell a-whoopin'." A thoughtful look in his eyes, Rimfire said, "She's got just one fault. When she gits out front she wants to wait for the competition."

Wishbone eyed him sharply. "That's a hell of a habit. Could lose us the race."

Rimfire nodded. "I'm workin' on it."

Horse Ketchum said, "We could use another hand around here."

"In most of the match races I ever saw," the half Navajo said, "nobody pays much attention to weight. Mostly the owners ride their own nags, but there's nothin' to say you can't ride whoever you want. And weight makes a difference. This feller Ashford prob'ly don't weigh more'n ninety pounds wet. Not one of us three — even countin' yourself — weighs less than one-forty. If we had a smart kid we could put up to ride —"

"I see what you mean," Wishbone said. "Where can we find one?"

"There's plenty young varmints around Tombstone," Flack said. "Question is, could you depend on them?"

"You could advertise in the papers, but that would be tipping your hand," Rimfire said. "You'd want a kid that looks raw, still wet behind the ears. That way, the difference in weight wouldn't look to make much difference."

"I'll study on it," Wishbone told them. "When you goin' to work this Whistlin' Cat filly?"

"About sunup tomorrow's her regular time. Nothin' to prevent her runnin' right now if you want to have a look at her. She's stout enough to do a couple four-forties a day without it botherin' her."

"Let's see this horse," Reilly said, so Horse Ketchum went off to fetch her.

Chacha Ronero came down from the house to see what they were up to. "When I was at home near Guadalajara I used to go out to the track to watch the horses work out," she said. "It kind of gets in your blood."

"It's sure got in mine," Rimfire said and grinned. "Nothin' I like better than a good horse race."

Horse Ketchum came up leading a well put together bay filly with a star and snip just below her forelock. The only other white showing was the patch just above her right hind hoof. "Isn't she beautiful?" Chacha said.

"It ain't her looks I'm interested in," Reilly answered. "What's her best lick?"

"Anything from three-fifty to six hundred and sixty yards," Rimfire said, "and long as I know eight or ten days in advance what distance the race is, I can have her ready. Like I said, she's a quick learner."

"She looks pretty eager right now," Wishbone commented.

"She's pretty high — feelin' her oats." The half Navajo grinned, his eyes lighting up. "When I get done with her she'll prob'ly look like she's been pulled through a knot hole. No use scarin' off the competition."

"What'll she do a quarter in?"

"About twenty-two four, but she can better that with a little encouragement."

"That's pretty fast," Chacha said. "Most of the horses I've watched couldn't lower twenty-two seven."

"There's one thing, though. You hit her with the bat and she goes off stride. Whoever we put on her has got to keep that in mind."

"I'll run the colt against her," Horse Ketchum said, kneeing Jaime into the right-hand stall.

After adjusting the stirrups, Rimfire climbed aboard the filly, and Flack broke open the gates. The filly came out like a bat out of hell. At the 220 pole she was a good length in the lead, but the colt was inching up. Even Reilly could see the filly wasn't happy running out there alone. The colt crept up and at about 350 they were neck and neck. The colt moved out. At about 400 yards he was half a length ahead. Flack muttered, "Forty yards to go." The filly bent to her work, came even wit'·

Jaime, then flattened her ears and finished a nose ahead.

They ran on out to the end of the track, swung round and loped back along the inside rail. "You catch the time?" Rimfire asked, and Flack said, "Twenty-two five."

"That's great!" Chacha cried. "And she could have lowered that."

Even Wishbone was impressed.

"She's very fast out of the gate," Rimfire said. "Biggest problem is she don't like running out there by herself. She's one of them come-from-behinders."

"That's a dang good way to lose," Wishbone growled.

"I've tried her with four different horses and," Rimfire said, staunch in his convictions, "she ain't lost yet."

"I dunno," Wishbone said. "Seems a pretty chancy business if you got money ridin' on her."

Horse Ketchum said, "I'm like Rimmy. I believe she can get the job done."

"What do you think? Shall we go on with her?" Reilly asked Chacha.

"If she were mine, I would."

Wishbone eyed her dubiously. "What's the best time you've got from them other two?" he asked Rimfire.

"Twenty-two six."

"That will beat most of them," Chacha said earnestly. "Twenty-two and six-tenths seconds has won a lot of match races in Mexico."

"You ever hold a stopwatch?"

"I always carried one when we went to the races."

"And you clocked winners at twenty-two six?" Wishbone asked skeptically.

"I certainly did," she said indignantly. "I know a lot more about this business than you do. I was brought up on it."

"Fair enough," Wishbone said with a laugh. "I ain't never pretended to be a racehorse man. Aside from ranchin' and minin' I'm a thick-headed duffer that don't know doodledee squat."

"I wouldn't go so far as to agree to that. Mostly, I think, you're just stubborn and obstinate. You latch on to a notion and nothing will budge you. I say Whistling Cat's the best filly you've got. And here's something else I've observed: eight times out of ten the mares and fillies in short races will outrun the horses. If you'd seen as many short races as I have, you'd know it's the geldings you've got to watch out for. In Mexico nobody wants to geld their horse colts."

"I thought Mex'kins was pretty handy with knives," Wishbone said; and Chacha, plainly offended, glared at him angrily. "That's a stupid remark! How would you like it if I said most of the gringos I've known liked nothing better than to get into a brawl?"

"I'd say most of the ones I've known would fit that shoe. Just the same, it's like sayin' the only good Injuns is dead ones — another old saw that's plumb wide of the mark." Reilly smiled at her indulgently. "I've prob'ly got knives on the brain right now. I was passin' the Atlantic in Tombstone the other day when one missed me by less than half a inch."

The girl's face paled, and she became visibly concerned. "I think you better stay away from there."

Wishbone hooted. "To hell with that! I been around a while. I can take care of what's mine, don't you worry," and he slapped the big pistol that hung at his hip.

"Boot Hill," Rimfire said, "is filled with people that held that belief."

"We better be walkin' these bangtails," Flack said. "Hot like they are, it won't do them much good to be standin' around."

Chapter Nineteen

When you start getting horses ready for the track, the days flit past like the fluff from milkweed. They found it hard to get around to all the things they had to do. Every day, the horses had to be taken out and exercised, ridden, broken out of the gates, worked on the track, legged up in sand to produce more muscle. A lot of folks don't subscribe to pampering horses, and Rimfire was not one to pamper anything; he did, however, feed Whistling Cat an occasional grapefruit, which she dearly loved.

Ashford showed up two or three times a week to break his sorrel-and-white "paint" gelding out of the gates, but he never ran him more than a few jumps before pulling him up. He'd keep breaking him out for an hour at a time and frequently hung around the track watching the Navajos work Reilly's prospects. About the only thing he wasn't privileged to see was Whistling Cat. Rimfire put her quickly out of sight whenever Ashford got within a mile of her. "Goddamn snoop!" the half

Navajo said, muttering as he rode his favorite back to the barn.

Men with horses were beginning to gather thick as cloves on a Christmas ham. One man brought a horse up from Mexico, a sleek black stallion that he called Lagrimas. A grulla gelding was fetched from Blythe, and two rival ranchers fetched runners from Sonoita, but most of the bangtails came from places like Tubac, Benson, Tucson and Willcox. There was one from Mammoth and two from Bagdad, all with high hopes.

It was when opening day was but two days away, with three matches to be run and both long rooms under the bleachers packed with the bedrolls of persons belonging to the Range Horse Breeders of America, that Chacha asked Reilly if he'd made a match for Whistling Cat.

"Hell no — ain't tried to match any of ours. I figure to see what we're up against first." He took hold of her arm. "One thing you can do is give me a kiss."

She shook off his hold and backed away.

"I thought you liked me," Wishbone growled.

"I like you well enough, but that kind of thing doesn't come free for the asking. Kisses have to be earned," she said coolly.

"Huh! I thought we were on better terms these days. What does a feller have to do to git into your good graces?" he asked in confusion.

She didn't back off, but her look turned wary, like she was ready to jump if he got out of hand. "You're too impetuous, too impatient. A girl likes to be courted if a man's truly serious."

"Ain't kissin' part of courtin'?"

"Comes in the later stages." She smiled and looked at him curiously. Reilly, it seemed to her, had of late taken on a harried expression, most likely the result of having too much on his mind, too many unaccustomed details to look after now that his prospective grand opening was only a couple of days away. "You've forgotten to provide a saddling paddock —" she began, hoping to change the subject.

"What do we need that for, with only two horses goin' at a time? I got enough to take care of without dreamin' up extras. What's botherin' me more'n anything's that dad-dratted Hannigan. You mark my words, he ain't through with us yet, not by a long shot."

"Are you charging the members for those rooms under the grandstand?"

"Well, I figured to, but Rimfire talked me out of it."

"Somebody asked me if we're planning a stud book."

"I got enough to take care of without registerin' bang-tails. What'd you tell them?"

"I told them I hadn't heard anything about one."

"You ain't goin' to, either. Cripes! With Hannah, Hannigan an' company breathin' down my neck, I'm about to wish I hadn't thought up this track. It's bringin' in a rough-lookin' crowd. Ashford tells me he's matched a race with some feller bringin' a horse up from Mexico — Eladio Gonzalez. You ever hear of him?"

She nodded. "He runs a stallion called Lagrimas. Black as coal."

"Any good?"

"I've never seen him run, but I know he's whipped a bunch of good horses. You say we're getting a rough-looking crowd. I notice you've been looking worried this last week or so. Do you think we'll have trouble at the track?"

"It ain't that," Wishbone said irritably. "Flack can take care of anythin' like that. I'm just wonderin' what devilment that damn Hannigan's up to. I expected that by now I'd be rid of him."

"I thought that riffraff Ives Hannah brought out here wiped out Hannigan's bunch."

"Well, they did. When he saw 'em cut down, he

skipped out, but now the two of 'em's teamed up to get me buried an' take over again. Wisht I knew what the hell they're hatchin'."

"You're expecting them to come out here during these races?"

"I've a hunch they're plannin' to wreck our track," Wishbone said, but what he actually had on his mind was far worse. He was scared they were counting on getting at him through her, which was why he had bought her that derringer. He would sooner give his right arm than have anything happen to Chacha Ronero, and Hannigan, he thought, was just about bright enough to understand that and to see in these races and the crowd they would draw a sure-fire opportunity. The feller had no more scruples than a hungry cougar!

"If you're really convinced there's some deviltry afoot, it seems Hannigan might try to involve Eladio Gonzalez in some way. So why don't we keep his horse in the barn and have Eladio come up and stay with us at the house?"

He was about to wave that aside when it occurred to him that having another man in the house was a pretty good notion, for she would be most vulnerable when she was alone, and there were bound to be times when he couldn't have his eye on her. "Well . . . if it would please you," he said; and then he thought of something that might please her even more. He smacked one fist into the palm of the other and said impulsively, "I'm going to give you Whistling Cat with no strings attached. She'll be your very own to do with as you please."

With wide-open eyes she searched his face and then smiled dazzlingly. "Oh Tom — do you mean it?" Still staring she said, "Truly?"

"Truly." He grinned, and she flung her arms around his neck. Pulling him close she gave him the kiss he'd been hoping for.

Chapter Twenty

But now that he'd got what he'd told her he wanted, he found there was no satisfaction in it. He'd given the filly freely, but it seemed the kiss was pay for the gift and that robbed him of its pleasure.

A strange rather startled look came over his face as he saw how she'd put it into his head to make her a gift of what was probably the best horse he had. He'd been a real chump, and it rankled. It wasn't that he begrudged her the filly, but the manner by which she'd acquired it made him look upon her with distrust.

Who'd put her up to it? Kisses, she'd said, must be earned. That really griped him. For wasn't *earned* just a fancier word for *bought*? She'd played him like a fool!

He completely forgot he'd been trying to get on the good side of her, and he showed up at the track with a chip on his shoulder and a black scowl on his face. He grabbed hold of Flack, a thing that hombre wouldn't ordinarily have allowed, but a glance at Reilly's expression turned Flack mute.

"Go find that damn Chink an' send him after the mail!"

With Flack starting off toward the bunkhouse and Lum Fung's domain, Reilly headed for where Rimfire and Horse Ketchum worked with the horses. "Well, are they ready?" he asked.

"About as ready as they ever will be, I guess," the half Navajo answered.

"What's the best lick for the best of that pair?"

Appearing somewhat surprised, Rimfire observed that the pair under discussion did not include Whistling Cat. "Well," he said, considering, "I've renamed them. I'm callin' that colt Potluck, and I believe he's a shade better at the quarter than Nellie Bly there. He'll make twenty-two six if he's pushed."

"See that he's pushed an' git him matched. We can't show off the value of our nags while they're standin' in a pen."

"If that's what you want," Horse Ketchum said, "you better match Whistling Cat."

"She's not mine to match," Wishbone said gruffly. "I've given her to Chacha."

Swinging round to start back to the house, he spied the girl talking with Ashford. Then the man beckoned him over. "Your housekeeper's been tryin' to talk me into matching Giddy Joe here against some filly she looks to be high on. Calls her Whistling Cat. You agreeable?"

"Sure. I'll put up the money. When's she want this affair to take place?"

"Sunday a week. Four hundred an' forty yards. What'll you put up?"

"What do you want?"

"I'd have to think in it. I don't run Joe for less'n five hundred," Ashford said, watching Reilly carefully.

"Sounds agreeable," Wishbone said. "Who's ridin' your horse?"

Ashford grinned. "Nobody rides Giddy Joe but me.

You can put anyone you want on the filly. You want to make a side bet?"

"Not today," Reilly said, and stomped off to the starting gates to confer again with Rimfire. Having given his trainer the facts of the matter, he said, "A boy on that filly might give us a little edge, make her fly faster."

"We ain't got no boy, nor time to train one if she's got that race set up for next Sunday. The Cat can take him easy as shootin' fish in a barrel."

Wanting to believe, but obviously skeptical, Reilly said, "Just remember whose *dinero* will be at risk." At this Rimfire let out an Indian chuckle. "That nag of Ashford's never saw the day he could outrun that filly at a quarter of a mile."

Bixby, the deputy U.S. marshal, arrived at Bullybueno that afternoon and announced he was ready to act as starter for the next day's races; a good many other folks were showing up too, and the number of people now prowling the grounds did nothing to improve Wishbone's disquieting hunch that tomorrow's gala opening would give Hannigan the chance that bugger had been waiting for.

He got Flack aside and gruffly told him to watch out for Chacha and keep an eye peeled for any sign of that villain. "He's bound to try to get back at me one way or another. He's the kind to my notion that won't stop at nothin'."

"Just what do you think he could do in this crowd?"

"Put a bullet through me if he gits half a chance," Wishbone growled. "But what I'm afraid of is he might try to get at me through my housekeeper. I don't want anything to happen to her."

Flack nodded. "I'll keep that in mind."

And on that note they parted, Flack to sift through the crowd while Wishbone followed his two hands with the horses back to the barn.

In the barn Horse Ketchum said, "No sign up till now of either Hannah or Hannigan, but we'll keep looking." And Rimfire said, "Why don't you get Potluck matched for a race tomorrow? That'll make four matched races and pack 'em in for our next meet."

Reilly, thinking it over, nodded. "All right, go ahead. See what you can do."

Early next morning Lum Fung got back from town with a burlap sack crammed with mail, and Wishbone sent him up to the house with orders to give it to Chacha and tell her to get busy on it. If all the mail was from people wanting to join his Horse Breeders association it might total up to as much as three or four hundred dollars, he thought excitedly.

While Wishbone was thinking about it, Flack joined him to ask, "How come you don't charge this crowd to watch these sprints? Must be close to five hundred people on tap right now, and we aren't even starting till one o'clock."

"I know. I thought about it, but Chacha didn't go for the notion. Said the more we pack in, the more we'll git next time."

"You oughta have programs with the names of the runners and owners. A couple bucks a head would pay for it. What you really need, though, is some kinda concession peddlin' eats and drinks. Or you could hire someone to take care of the stand. It could bring in some real money."

"Dang my soul if you ain't plumb right. We'll see if we can't work somethin' out," Wishbone said enthusiastically. Food an' stogies — great idea."

As he was turning away, a man with mutton-chop whiskers, wearing an elegant pearl-gray derby, came up to him, saying, "I understand you've got horses for sale. Any race prospects?"

"They're all race prospects, though some I reckon is

better than others. Run's been bred into all of 'em. We'll probably be runnin' one this afternoon if we can get him matched."

"That the only one you've got ready?"

"No, we've got a filly named Nellie Bly which ought to go four-forty in twenty-two six or better. If you're interested, go along up to the barn an' have Rimfire, my trainer, give you a look at her."

"How much you asking?"

"Wasn't plannin' to sell her, but if you'll take her today I'll let you have her for a thousand dollars, cash in my hand."

The granite-jawed man looked a bit skeptical. But as he turned away another gent in an open leather vest came up to ask if Reilly was owner of this spread. Once assured that such was the case, he said breathlessly, "You know who that was? That feller's the castings king, Benjamin P. Dalton! Got a big foundry in Pittsburg. Reason I know is we're both staying at the Pioneer Hotel in Tucson. He's a nut about sprinters, short horses. You got any more you'd let go of?"

"Don't believe I caught your name," Reilly said.

"Pete Quintares. I'm trainer for a big hacienda south of Nogales. Owner's interested in match racing. When Dalton told me he was coming out here I figured what was good enough for him would suit my boss, too. All right for me to go look at that filly?"

"By grab," Wishbone said, "there's no charge for lookin'. Got a horse colt I'll sell you that's already in trainin'. He's booked to run today."

Quintares shook his head. "In my experience a good filly will outrun most of the good colts. Don't ask me why 'cause I don't know, but they generally will."

"Come along," Wishbone said. "I got a penful of prospects you can train to suit yourself." Then he headed for the day pen and the bangtails Horse Ketchum had fetched in off the range a couple weeks earlier

On reaching the pen Quintares peered through the poles and took a good long look. "Let's see that gray filly — that flea-bitten one," he finally said.

So Reilly grabbed up a halter, went in and led her out, walking her around to give Quintares a chance to examine her action. The man nodded. "What's the price?"

Wishbone, encouraged by his conversation with Dalton, said, "Ten hundred bucks."

The Mexican looked at him sourly. "That's what you told Dalton for a nag that was ready to run."

"Take it or leave it."

"Let's see that *bayo coyote*."

Wishbone put the gray back in the pen and led out a dun-colored filly with dark markings above and below the knees and hock joints, and an equally dark stripe along her spine. Quintares led this one around himself. Looking at her teeth, he said, "If you're asking the same for this one I'll take them both."

"I got no time to be deliverin' bangtails," Wishbone said, "but if you'll take 'em yourself right here an' now it's a deal."

"I'll take them," the hacienda man said, fetched out his roll and peeled off two yellow-backed thousand dollar bills which he put into Reilly's hand.

Wishbone was passing the already-filled bleachers heading toward the track when Benjamin P. Dalton in his derby, with a stogie in the corner of his mouth, came hurrying after him. "Hold on there, Reilly! At nine hundred I'll take that Nellie Bly filly off your hands."

"Ha! Ha!" Reilly grinned. "I'm a one-price man, except that if I put her into that match — win, lose or draw — her ticket will be two thousand flat."

The Pittsburg castings king gave him a scowl no red-blooded man would have cared for, reluctantly shoved a hand in his pocket and came up with the tab. "Write me out a receipt," he growled. "Chacha Ronero takes care

"Chacha Ronero takes care of the paper work — you'll find her up at the house," Wishbone said, and headed for the starting gates to confer with Bixby.

But, partway there, it crossed his mind that Chacha was probably alone up there at the house and, swinging round, he set off in Dalton's wake, his big bone-handled pistol bobbing at his hip. It didn't pay to get careless.

When he got back to the house he realized he needn't have worried, for Jack Flack was there with his butt to the veranda railing alongside of Good Eye.

Chapter Twenty-One

By twenty minutes to one the bleachers were crammed to capacity and a dense throng of people was jostling one other trying to get a good view. Seemed like every man and his uncle for a hundred miles in all directions had found their way into Bullybueno to witness Reilly's spectacle.

There were big hats and bonnets, picture hats and derbies, even a scattering of caps and headbands. Persons garbed in everything save breechclouts were all squeezed together and jabbering like magpies. Bixby had the crowd figured at more than 700.

Promptly at twenty after one the first pair of starters went into the closed stalls. Without fooling around, Bixby yelled "Now!" and hauled back the lever.

The gates banged open and Buckskin Bill and Mitzy Canello plunged into their lanes as though flung from a catapult, their riders squatting in the stirrups and the spectators screaming their heads off. Nothing like a horse race to agitate a crowd from the great open spaces,

Wishbone thought. This match had been billed as a full quarter-miler, and the colt was in front at the eighth pole by half a head. His supporters roared encouragement. At 350 the filly was leading by a full neck and it certainly looked like she was drawing away. But at the 400 mark the colt surged ahead and went on to win handily.

"Wasn't quite up to it," Bixby said as though following the turn Reilly's thoughts had taken. "Pretty good, but not good enough." He held up the stopwatch. "Twenty-two eight."

The colt's winning backers were having a jubilee. In the midst of this, Wishbone, peering about, noticed a small but growing gathering of gawkers off near the sealed far end of the stands. And, just as this caught his attention, Chacha came up from the opposite direction to ask, "Did you sell Nellie Bly?"

Reilly grinned. "For a thousand. Did you fix up a receipt for that hard-hatted hombre?" When she nodded, he said, "An' how about that bagful of mail I sent up to the house?"

She laughed. "As you Anglos say, 'all saucered and blowed.'" Then with a frown between her dark eyes she cried, "What's going on over there?" Wishbone spun around and left on the run to find out.

As he came up on a five-deep circle of onlookers, he heard the sound of angry voices. Forcing his way through he found Flack confronting an obstreperous Ives Hannah. Flack was saying through the man's defiant splutter, "You can go feet first if that's the way you want it."

Staring, furious, Hannah licked at dry lips, abruptly turned on his heels and strode off toward the Bullybueno entrance gate, where a lone horse was tethered to one of the uprights. "Don't let me see you round here again," Flack called after him as the onlookers hissed at the man in derision.

Reilly nodded to Flack and made his way back to Chacha Ronero. Horses were now being loaded for the second match, a 400-yard go. "Nellie Bly's in this one against a filly called Wasp," she said. "Oh, I do hope she'll win!"

"Yeah," Wishbone grunted. "Dalton won't much like it if she don't get there first."

The tailgates closed with a bang. Bixby yelled, "Go!" and the two fillies burst into their lanes and went streaking for the finish neck and neck, their pounding hoofs kicking up the dust. Nellie Bly, with Rimfire aboard, got her nose out in front about two yards from the finish and still had it there when they tore across the line.

While the winners went about collecting their bets and Bixby was counting the stakes posted by the owners into the hand of Benjamin P. Dalton, Reilly's delighted housekeeper, catching hold of his arm, cried, "She did it! She did it! That ought to prove we've got a penful of good ones!"

Wishbone grinned. "Been a hell of a thing if she'd lost that match."

But his mind wasn't really on it. He couldn't rid himself of the memory of Ives Hannah stalking off toward his mount, his face contorted with rage. He spent the next twenty minutes prowling round through the crowd looking for Hannigan, but to no avail. Probably the fellow wasn't here, Wishbone tried to reassure himself, but it didn't work.

The day's third match was now being readied. Bullybueno's Potluck was to run against a mare called Hardtime Maybel. Wishbone had put up $400 with no bets on the side.

Potluck, with Rimfire up, looked to be in good shape and was obviously eager. The mare looked calm as they went into the gates, about half asleep it looked like to Reilly, who was beginning to regret not having placed any bets on behalf of his colt. But Chacha, observing both contestants, said, "I hope you haven't gone overboard; I've seen that look on short horses before. I'll bet you that Maybel's a miniature whirlwind," and as the race unfolded, Reilly's housekeeper was proved emphatically right.

They both got off well, the colt slightly in the lead but with the mare inching up. At the halfway mark they were running dead even. Then the mare pulled away, and from that point on continued widening her lead until at the finish she crossed the line a full length ahead of Potluck, apparently coasting.

Reilly swore, but Chacha only laughed. "That colt's all right. He was just overmatched. That sleepy-looking Maybel had speed to spare."

Just the same, it shook Reilly's faith in Rimfire's judgment. He decided next time he ran one of his bangtails he'd let Chacha do the matching.

It was crowding four o'clock when the featured race of the day was loaded into the starting gates, Ashford's Giddy Joe versus Eladio Gonzalez's sleek black Mexican stallion, Lagrimas. The Mexican horse was a beauty, no doubt about it. But as one ranchman not far from Reilly remarked, "Looks don't mean nothing. My money's on the paint." Wishbone thought this pretty remarkable since most of the cowmen he had known had little use for pintos.

When the gates burst open, Lagrimas took the lead. This was for three furlongs, the length of Reilly's track. At the 220, Lagrimas was ahead by half a length and the crowd, as though shocked, was utterly quiet, staring incredulously as the horses passed the 350 marker with Lagrimas far in the lead. You could hear a few groans through the sound of hoofs. Then Ashford's paint began to close the gap, and at the quarter mile post Ashford's Giddy Joe wasn't half a length back. In the bleachers the onlookers were all on their feet, yelling their encouragement as Giddy Joe's head came even with the black stallion's withers. At 600 the pair were running neck and neck and the crowd went wild as Giddy Joe took the lead by a nose, lost it, regained it and crossed the finish a full head the best.

You could have heard the racket halfway to Tucson.

Chapter Twenty-Two

Catching hold of his arm Chacha hauled Wishbone over
to where Deputy Marshal Bixby stood leaning against
the starting gates. He left off putting together a smoke
and straightened. Then he put on his twisted smile and
doffed his hat. "You're looking cheerful," he said to Reilly's companion. "You win a big bet on one of them
bangtails?"

"No." She grinned. "I just love to watch them run."

"What was the time on that last one?" Reilly asked.

"Forgot to start my watch," Bixby said. "Looked
pretty fast."

"We'll just stay here with you until Ashford shows up
for his winnings," said Chacha. "I'd like to match my
filly, Whistling Cat — we call her Kitty — against Mr.
Ashford's paint."

Bixby whistled. "I admire your nerve. That horse is an
old campaigner and Ashford's up to every trick in the
book."

"Well," Chacha said, "Lagrimas had Giddy Joe pretty

well extended. I'm sure Kitty can do better than that at six-sixty."

Bixby looked at her curiously. "Is that just a hunch or do you know it for sure?"

"What's sure in this world?" she asked, grinning back at him.

"Here he comes now," Bixby said.

She turned as Ashford came up to them leading his skewbald gelding. Bixby handed over the money Giddy Joe had won, and Chacha asked, "Have you decided to match Giddy Joe against my filly?"

"Depends. What distance do you have in mind?"

"Same one he ran today, three furlongs."

Bixby reckoned Ashford would want at least to have a look at the filly, but all the man said was, "For how much and when?"

"Next Sunday afternoon," the girl answered and tossed a challenging look at Reilly, who said, "I'm backing her. Will a thousand suit you?"

"Make it fifteen hundred and you've got a match."

"Done," Wishbone said, and the two men shook hands on it.

Having witnessed the last race for the day, the chattering crowd had by now pretty well dispersed. Ashford went to cool off his gelding before picking up his saddle horse to head for home. Chacha and Reilly had a few more words with Bixby then headed for the house. When they reached the yard they saw Horse Ketchum and a glum-looking Rimfire walking Potluck around the barn. Wishbone beckoned Horse Ketchum, while Chacha ran over to tell Rimfire about matching her filly against Giddy Joe.

"I've got a sackful of mail in the office and a packet of checks and paper money I want to get banked. You feel like ridin' in to town after dinner?"

"Sure thing. I'll try an' be back before dark tomorrow."

"Good," Wishbone muttered and, struck by a sudden

thought, broke into a run toward the track, hoping to catch Bixby before he departed.

"What's ailin' you?" the deputy asked in astonishment when Wishbone arrived.

"Wanted to ask if you knew my uncle," Wishbone said, panting.

"Cornelious? Sure. I expect most everyone in these parts knew him."

"I can't recollect too much about him, not havin' seen him in more'n twenty years," Wishbone said. "What was he like?"

"Like? Depends on which side of him you stood. To friends, old Cornelious was like a rock. To enemies, I'd call him a damn rough character. Never one to forget a friend or give any quarter to an enemy. What bee's buzzin' round in your bonnet?"

"Did you know he had a mine?" Wishbone asked, and Bixby's stare turned thoughtful.

"Seems like a good while ago I did hear somethin' of that nature. What about it?"

"You got any idea where it was located?"

"I can tell you this: if he had a mine, he wasn't the sort to give out such information. Mighty reticent sort was Cornelious."

"Lawyer feller in Hermosillo told me he had this unrecorded mine. If it's round here someplace, I'd kinda like to git hold of it."

"Guess a lot of folks would. Sorry I can't help you. Seemed to me it was mostly talk, but *if* he had one and never recorded it, my best advice to you is forget it. That ol' boy was cagey as a Injun."

It seemed suddenly important to Reilly to find Cornelious's mine if the old man had truly had one. Didn't seem possible in this kind of country, filled as it was with rogues and villains of an almost infinite variety, to keep a mine of any magnitude concealed. Still, a crusty old

Dutchman was said to have hidden one so well somewhere up in the Superstitions it never had been found.
So why not Cornelious who, according to repute, had
lived like feudal robber baron, riding roughshod over
everything in sight?

Reilly had actually already done a little bit of looking,
but now that he was thinking about it seriously the most
likely place to conduct a real search seemed to be up in
those wooded hills north of headquarters. It was those
unrewarding years of prospecting the Sonoran deserts
and adjacent mountains, he guessed, that had all of a
sudden made him want to seek out this treasure.

Horse Ketchum came back from town with another
big sack of mail addressed to the Range Horse Breeders
and a liberal supply of gossip, mostly involving exagger-
ated reports of the Bullybueno match race. All of it was
grist for Wishbone's mill.

That afternoon when they went through the mail
Horse Ketchum had fetched Chacha discovered twenty
letters with Mexican stamps, eight of them from breed-
ing establishments like the hacienda she had come from.
There was a total of 119 pieces of mail, all having to do
either with the track or his range horse registry. One
hundred and eight of the writers enclosed either checks
or currency.

Despite this bonanza Reilly prowled the hills for the
next three days unsuccessfully trying to pin down the
location of Cornelious's mine — if, indeed, there was
one.

With the next race just three days away he was forced
to quit that pipe dream and work with the others in
readying Whistling Cat for her debut as a sprinter. Roust-
abouts from Tombstone had brought out enough lumber
and supplies to set up the food and drink stand Bixby
had suggested; and Wishbone had hired a girl from Tucson to preside at this concession with the help of Lum

Fung and of Chacha whenever she wasn't fussing over Whistling Cat.

It was fall and the Arizona Territory was basking in the finest of Indian summer weather on the Sunday of the second Bullybueno race. The grounds between the main gate and the house had all the appearance of a gold stampede. The outer fringes were decorated with the tents of early arrivals, including several wigwams and hogans. And there were, of course, enough tethered horses to mount a cavalry regiment.

Five races had been booked, and betting was heavy; touts and bookies were doing a flourishing business. Several fights broke out and were quickly quelled when the combatants discovered Jack Flack was there to keep the peace, for Jack had a wide and quite ominous reputation throughout the territory. It was astonishing to see how folks fell back when he came stalking in their direction.

The big attraction billed for this occasion was Ashford's Giddy Joe, known as practically a sure thing in any match he showed up for. If you were betting on Giddy Joe to win, you had to give all the odds to those who bet against him, and such fools were almost as scarce as hen's teeth.

To make the odds even better, Reilly had arranged to keep Kitty out of sight until the match was called.

Bullybueno had no other horse running at this second meet. Wishbone's concession stand was doing a land-office business with an almost constant attendance of ravenous customers six and eight deep.

The first four races went off without a hitch with Bixby and Flack keeping the noisy throngs under continual scrutiny. Neither Hannah nor Hannigan appeared to be in evidence, though Reilly wasn't one to accept appearances for fact.

At last the featured race was called, the Giddy Joe–Whistling Cat match. Seemed like everyone was craning their necks to get a look at the brash filly some fool woman had been crazy enough to run against the region's champ sprinter.

Chacha had woven a little pink bow into the fluff of top hair just over the filly's eyes, and more than a few derisive snorts and ribald comments greeted Rimfire's appearance on her in breechclout and bare feet, without saddle and with nothing to hang on to but a surcingle.

Ashford sneered at this spectacle, but among the resounding hoots and laughter an intent listener might have caught a few faint bravos. Rimfire, sitting stoically erect, paid no more heed to the one than the other but reined the Cat over and into the starting gate as Ashford fetched his own horse up.

Bixby, after making certain both animals were in position and ready, wasted no time on amenities. "Go!" he yelled, and hauled back the lever.

The gates flew open with a bang, both contestants bursting into their lanes. On her third jump the Cat, with half a length lead, politely eased till Joe caught up.

Reilly swore, Chacha looked anxious; the crowd roared as the paint surged ahead.

At the eighth pole it was Giddy Joe by a length and going strong. "Wake up you fool!" Wishbone shouted. "Git the goddamn lead out!" Chacha's eyes looked big as saucers.

At the 350 marker Whistling Cat was creeping up. At 400 yards they were neck and neck, apparently going all out, their ears flattened, their forelocks flying.

But as they passed the quarter mile the paint began to draw away, opening up another half-length lead, and Reilly shut his eyes in disgust. But when Chacha dug her fingers into his arm he jerked his eyes open to find the filly with her whole neck ahead. At 550 she was in the lead by a quarter. With the finish pole not a hundred yards ahead of him Giddy Joe made his final bid with

Ashford swinging his bat frantically. For about two jumps he got his head out in front, then the filly swept past and crossed the line, nostrils flaring, winner by a nose and handful of whiskers.

Chapter Twenty-Three

So Chacha's faith in Whistling Cat was vindicated.

There wasn't a great deal of noise from the crowd; too many people had plunked their money on what they'd considered to be a sure thing and didn't like losing it. But the few whose financial position had taken a leap for the better were yelling themselves hoarse. Eyes bright, Wishbone jumped up and down in excitement, and Chacha, still clinging to his arm, was doing the same, positively screaming in the flush of her horse's triumph.

It was not much later when Ashford came up to them cool as you please to say, "Well, that's that. Congratulations, Miss Ronero. How would you like to do it again?"

She stared at him. "You're proposing another match? You're thinking, Mr. Ashford, this was a fluke?"

"Well, I have to consider that possibility, you know. Why don't we try this again? Same terms, same distance? Two weeks from today?"

"That's great," she said with obvious enthusiasm. "I'd be delighted."

"Don't suppose," Ashford queried, "you'd care to double the stakes?"

"Why not?" Wishbone grinned. "Let's do it!" he cried.

But Chacha, eyeing a scrape that looked like a stone bruise across the front of the paint's left hind foot, was more inclined to be cautious. "Are you sure," she asked Reilly, "you want to risk that much? Perhaps Giddy Joe wasn't up to his best."

"Hoo hoo!" Wishbone jeered. "Nag never saw the day he could beat our Kitty! You're on," he told Ashford. "Two weeks from today — same distance. Three thousand a side!"

"Good," Ashford said, and went off with his gelding to cool him out.

Rimfire, Chacha thought, when told of the rematch seemed less than enthusiastic, but if he had reservations he did not mention them and went on with his work of rubbing the Cat down.

Bixby came up and gave Wishbone his winnings including the track's percentage. "Quite a race," he said and chuckled. "When word of this rematch gets around I dunno's we'll have room enough to hold everyone. Be packin' them in like sardines I reckon. Better charge to see this one."

"Well," Chacha said reluctantly, "perhaps a dollar a head would be all right."

Reilly glanced at the deputy. "Want I should git a batch of tickets printed up?"

"Good idea. Better collect at the gate. Say, you took in quite a bundle with that food."

A grinning Horse Ketchum said, "Mebbe we oughta put in for a raise."

"You'll have it," declared Wishbone as though this were Christmas.

It was just about then that he recalled sending Horse

Ketchum to town with the outgoing mail and the checks and cash to be banked. "You have any problem while you were in Tombstone?"

"Nope. Not a one. Banked your money, sent off them letters and picked up half a sack of Horse Breeders mail. I put it all in your office."

"Fine," Wishbone said and headed for the house, the girl almost running in an attempt to keep up with him.

"What's the rush?" she gasped, and Reilly slowed up a mite.

"I dunno — just my way I guess. Sorry." What he didn't tell her was that once again he was worrying that while they were all taken up with the match race Hannah, Hannigan and company could have got into the house and raised all kinds of hell.

But they hadn't, apparently. Nothing, as he remembered it, seemed to be out of place when they'd arrived. "Better get at that sack of mail," he told her, and went off to have a look in the bunkhouse, the dog going with him.

Another week dragged itself past without fresh problems. Wishbone and all the others at the Bullybueno spent most of their time either working with Kitty, offering advice or just sitting around watching. She seemed to be in good shape, and even Rimfire conceded that he could find no real reason for her not to beat Giddy Joe again. "There's just one thing," he said, "that sticks in my craw: I kin understand Ashford not being convinced — as Chacha said, he probably figures that was a fluke or his horse wasn't up to his best lick that day — but," he said, scowling, "the risk is all his, so why raise the ante?"

"Wants to git back what he lost," Wishbone said, but his half Navajo trainer continued to look doubtful.

It was at this point that Chacha, peering toward the gate, said, "Looks like we're about to have company."

Reilly, turning, saw a man on horseback approach with a packhorse in tow. "Anyone seen that feller before?" They all shook their heads.

"Hope I'm not interrupting anything," the stranger said, pulling up before them. "My name's Larkin. I travel for the Sunburst Plant an' Seed Company out of El Paso. On this trip, in the hope of stimulating a little new business, I'm empowered to give away — just one to each customer — a very decorative fly-catcher plant. No, you don't have to buy a thing. If you enjoy your plant, perhaps next time I make this trip you might wish to order several or perhaps something else. We carry a full line of plants plus all sorts of seeds. Vegetables, flowers, shrubs — the whole line."

"What's a fly-catcher plant?" Chacha asked curiously.

"May I get down?" asked the man.

"Sure," Wishbone said, and once the man dismounted, he stepped over to the horse he had on a lead shank, opened up his pack and brought out a small flowerpot that was nearly filled with dirt. "It's a dry-weather plant, grows best in arid climates. In two or three days it'll push up through the dirt. They're just plumb beautiful," he said.

"But what do they look like? Do they have any purpose other than being ornamental?" Chacha inquired.

"Yes, ma'am, indeed they have. They'll rid your house of flies in no time. As for how they look . . . Well, they produce a pod that when it's ripe opens up to reveal a sort of whiskery interior . . . something like an orchid. It's got half a dozen colors and the flies go after them just like it's honey. Then the pod closes up and smothers the little devils."

"And you're going to give me a sample?"

"Yes, ma'am — free, gratis, no charge of any kind. Good will's what we're hunting in the hope of a nice order next time." He smiled. "Does best if you don't water it," he said, handing her the pot. "Just keep it where it'll be reasonably warm. Most folks keep them where they do their eating. Keeps down the flies you know. Better than flypaper and a whole lot prettier."

"Thank you so much," Chacha said, looking pleased. "I'll take good care of it."

Chapter Twenty-Four

Since she didn't think it seemly for the heir to Bully-bueno to have to eat in the kitchen like a common hand, Chacha and Wishbone took their meals in the room old Cornelious had used for that purpose. So this was where she took the wonder plant, setting the little pot down among the other things she was growing in tomato tins on the sill of the window overlooking the yard.

Remembering the salesman's glowing description, she could hardly wait for the magical thing to come up, grow its pod and start catching flies. It was the first thing she looked for the following morning. But the soil in the pot was still undisturbed and was still smooth at noon. Not even the tiniest tendril had pushed itself up when they sat down to supper.

"Prob'ly a dud," Wishbone said with a sniff. "Anytime you git somethin' for nothin' in this world you can hang out the flag!"

"Oh, I don't know. The man said it might take two or three days to come up," Chacha reminded him, wrinkling her nose. "Haven't I heard you Anglos say Rome wasn't built in a day?"

"Expect that's one of them Navajo saws, like old Gabe fiddlin' while Nero blew his trumpet."

That did not sound quite right, she thought, but what could one expect of a gringo barbarian? Crude though he was and frequently vulgar, stingy at times and occasionally phenomenally generous, she was not immune to his boyish attitudes. She doubted that Wishbone could ever be the man of her dreams, but sometimes she felt that with proper handling he might come to be considerably more than her means of survival.

His recklessness, though it often frightened her, was easier to bear than his boastful cocksureness or his deplorable tendency to ride roughshod over people. But what did it matter? She might as well admit that with all his drawbacks he was the only man she knew with whom she could contemplate a future. A stormy one certainly, but wasn't that a part of his attraction? She had never known anyone like him.

Once again Lum Fung returned from town with a big load of groceries, including more fodder for the concession stand, three sacks of oats for the horses in training, two blocks of salt, and more mail for the Horse Breeders.

Two ranchers with spreads in the vicinity of Tucson had come out and bought horses on the strength of Kitty's victory over Giddy Joe. And one gent from as far off as Blythe had bought a stud colt for $2,500. Also, a *hacendado* from Chihuahua who'd been visiting in Cortaro had purchased a mare by Zantanon that Chacha had told Reilly not to sell. But the man was determined to have her and put down $4,000 in cash before Wishbone gave in and let him depart with her.

With the fateful Sunday but two days away and a roll in his pocket big enough to choke a horse, Wishbone Reilly, master of Bullybueno, in his *charro* clothes and red sombrero surveyed his world and found it much to his liking. Only Rimfire still went around with a frown on his face.

"I don't like any part of this deal," he told Horse Ketchum on Saturday night. "The Cat's in fine shape, can't fault her on any count except for that damnable habit she's got of easin' up when she's ahead, and I believe I've got that whipped at last. What I can't git over is feelin' that swivel-eyed polecat's got somethin' up his sleeve."

"You talking about Ashford?"

"You know it," Rimfire growled. "I've worked my tail off gettin' the Cat ready an' I know deep down in my bones she's got no more chance of winnin' this race than you got of findin' hair on a frog!"

"I'm puttin' my money on her," Horse Ketchum told him with a tolerant grin. "If she's kicked that damn habit, you got nothing to worry about. Bettin' her to win, ain't you?"

"No I ain't!"

Horse Ketchum peered at him questioningly. "Better not let the boss hear that. He might git the notion you're throwin' this race."

"You know me better'n that!" Rimfire snarled.

"Wouldn't be the first time a trainer's been bribed."

The half Navajo bristled like he wanted to slam five knuckles against his friend's jaw. Then he went stomping off like a wet-footed tom, grinding his chompers hard enough to break them.

Horse Ketchum, looking after him, shook his head. Nerves in a man he'd never known to show any made him decide to keep his money in his pocket. He didn't believe his friend had been bought off, but it seemed to him, in the face of Rimfire's conviction, that his money would be safest right where it was.

Sunday dawned with an overcast sky and got Wishbone

to wondering what a drizzle might to do Whistling Cat's performance. They'd never worked her in the rain. There hadn't been any since they'd put her in training. Some nags, he knew, didn't like to run in mud, and she might be one of them.

With a whopping crowd already on hand despite the newly inaugurated dollar-a-head charge, he decided to have a few words with Ashford and cornered him walking Giddy Joe behind the stands. "Reckon we're in for some rain?" he asked.

Ashford took a squint at the sky and shook his head. "Don't think so. Ain't the season for rain."

Still scowling, Wishbone said, "How would you feel about puttin' this match of ours first on the ticket?"

"If you're worryin' about it, I've no objection. Go ahead an' put it first if it'll make you feel any better."

"Think I will," Reilly growled, and went off to find Bixby.

"How many matches have we got today?" he asked the deputy marshal.

"Five again," Bixby said, "and five have already been arranged for next Sunday. And three the week after. What's on your mind?"

"You got any objection to puttin' Whistling Cat an' Giddy Joe first?"

Bixby studied on it. "Ain't going to rain if that's what's botherin' you. Sure ain't customary to put the feature first. You talked to Ashford?"

Wishbone nodded. "He's agreeable."

"Trouble is," Bixby told him, "there'll be a hell of a lot of people comin' out here just to see Giddy Joe whip your filly, and most of them, carin' nothing about the rest of it, won't be gettin' here till the afternoon's half gone." He considered Reilly earnestly. "I don't think we better. Goin' to be a heap of hard feelin's if we run that pair first."

Wishbone chewed on his lip, not sure what to do, but

finally, clenching his jaw, said, "All right, run it last," and walked off muttering to himself.

Oddly enough, it wasn't the possible loss of his money that had put Wishbone into such an unaccustomed sweat. He could stand that now — or leastways he thought he could. It was his long-standing worry about Hannigan and the fellow's lack of any all-out effort to even the score that was giving Wishbone the screaming jeebies. From what he'd heard of that gunslinging bastard, it wasn't like Hannigan to drag his feet after coming off with the short end of the stick. And all he'd done so far hadn't amounted to a hill of beans even if you credited him with Uncle's "promised bride," the IOU's, the rascal who claimed he'd not been paid for a stud horse and the various ambush attempts which hadn't come off.

You had to consider the fellow's frightful reputation, which must have been damaged when he was driven off of Bullybueno, Wishbone thought. You wouldn't think he could stand such a loss of face too long without going all out to redeem it.

He had to be waiting for the right opportunity, and Wishbone still believed that devil was waiting for the chance to strike at him through Chacha. It just about shriveled Reilly's soul to realize the extreme vulnerability in his chain of defenses represented by this girl he had come to value above all his possessions. With each passing hour it appeared more certain to Wishbone that Chacha just had to be Hannigan's target.

He had confided this awful conviction to at least one of the Navajos as well as to Bixby. But the deputy marshal had made light of his fears. "Not likely," said Bixby. "In this country, Reilly, molesting a woman is the most heinous crime a man can be charged with. Why, these folks around here would boil him in tar if they even suspected he would try such a thing!"

But this assurance did little to get Wishbone's mind

off the notion. He'd said as much to Jack Flack, his hired gun, and bade the man keep both his eyes peeled. But Hannah's showing up at the track last Sunday had fetched all Reilly's fears back in a rush. He couldn't even honestly count on Good Eye to protect her for, according to Chacha, "That dog's got you down for an easy mark! All the food you pour into him — *Madre de Dios*! He bristles all up and growls if he reckons that's what you're expecting. It's the only exertion you can look for from him!"

"What about that IOU feller he chased into his buggy?"

"He only did that because the stupid fool ran."

"He grabbed a mouthful of cloth from the seat of his pants —"

"What's that got to do with anything? If that gringo had turned to shake a fist at him, he'd have run for cover!"

What man ever got anyplace arguing with a woman?

The first match, as advertised in the Tombstone papers, was loaded into the starting gates at one o'clock promptly. Bixby yelled, the gates flew open and the first pair of sprinters sprang into their lanes. A gelding was racing against a three-year-old filly, who was badly overmatched and plainly outclassed. She couldn't even keep up, and the gelding won by two and a half lengths. As a spectator sport it was a washout.

Twenty minutes later the next pair went at it. The horses were pretty evenly matched, but the rider of the winner was some sixty pounds lighter than his opponent, and his defeated rival had been unable to overcome the difference in weight

There was considerable grumbling among the onlookers, a good many of whom felt they weren't getting their money's worth. Bixby shrugged. "We only furnish the track. We make no rules about riders or weights. That's up to the owners. If one of 'em's fool enough to give away that much weight, it's not our concern."

Someone said something about a kid in three-cornered pants knowing better than to expect a nag to win against such odds. And those without seats continued to mill around grumbling and cussing about coming so far and being soaked a dollar to watch a horse get clobbered in that fashion. Some hothead yelled "It oughtn't to be allowed!"

The next two races went off somewhat better, and at last it was time for the advertised feature, the rematch between Giddy Joe and Whistling Cat, the contest that had drawn the biggest share of the crowd.

Ashford climbed aboard his gelding, and Wishbone noticed that, instead of the stock saddle he'd used the first time, all he had between himself and Giddy Joe was the same sort of surcingle the half Navajo was using; but unlike Rimfire, he had all his clothes on and was looking pretty complacent, as if he were certain to win. Rimfire looked badly worried but determined.

With both horses ready, Kitty champing at her bit, Bixby hauled back the lever and yelled, "Now!" and the pair charged out of the gates. Neck and neck they plunged down the lanes, first one a bit ahead then falling slightly behind the other. At the 350 marker Giddy Joe had the lead by nearly a quarter of a length and the crowd went wild, shouting loud enough to wake the dead. Then the Cat laid her ears back and streaked past Giddy Joe to a three-quarters lead.

Ashford went to the bat, and the way he was banging it against poor Joe told better than words what kind of frenzy he was in. Under this pummeling Giddy Joe crept up to Kitty's withers where he seemed to hang as though locked in place.

With but sixty yards of track left ahead of them Whistling Cat began to fade and the crowd took up their yelling again. Everyone in the stands was on his feet. The Cat was still leading, but by barely half a head; to Wishbone it looked more like a diminishing nose.

When they crossed the finish, where Jack Flack stood, Giddy Joe inched his lip out in front and won by three inches — Flack said a nostril. But whatever it was, it left the heir to Bullybueno stripped of close to $6,000.

Chapter Twenty-Five

Losing that much money in less than two minutes was enough of a shock to unnerve most anyone. Wishbone was still standing around like he'd been kicked in the belly when Ashford, hunting for Bixby in order to collect his winnings, came up to Wishbone. "Just goes to show," he said smiling smugly, "what happens to amateurs when they go up against a professional. Hope that'll be a lesson to you, Reilly."

"Nope," Wishbone growled. "I ain't convinced yet."

"Well," Ashford said with a laugh, "some people never learn. If I hadn't held Joe back he'd have run plumb away from your filly."

Wishbone bristled at this obvious lie. "Yeah?"

"Sounds like you're honin' for another crack at Joe."

Wishbone, seething, said impulsively, "You bet. We got a full card next Sunday, but Sunday a week, if you believe what you're sayin', I'd be proud to take another whack at him. Same distance, and we'll feature it in the papers."

Ashford looked like he couldn't believe what he was hearing, just couldn't believe he'd met up with such a fool. "You ain't serious, are you?"

"You think I'm talkin' just to hear my head rattle? Two wins outa three ought to prove something. Go on, name the stakes if you're so sure you've got a world beater. Put your money where your mouth is."

Ashford looked him over like he was hunting for the joker. "It ain't that I mind takin' your money, but if I have to go through all this again, let's make it worthwhile —"

He broke off as Chacha and Flack came up with them. "What are you two up to?" the girl asked, staring suspiciously from one to the other. "Not trying to work up another a rematch I hope." She eyed Reilly like she thought he didn't have sense enough to know dung from wild honey. Which was the wrong tack to take with a fellow like Wishbone who hadn't ever yet backed away from a dare.

"You know well as I do how we lost that race. She just can't stand being out there by herself!" he stated, and Flack said, "She had that race won when she started easin' up, hardly more'n one jump from the finish."

Ashford asked, "Is that what it was? I reckoned she'd give out."

"She don't ever give out." Wishbone glared belligerently. "Come on — what'll you run for?"

"In that case, how's about fifty thousand?" Ashford said like he'd stock in the mint.

Staring at him incredulously Reilly said, "I ain't got that much."

"You've got a ranch you could put up," Ashford told him and it got so quiet you could hear the locusts in the hackberry trees half a mile away. Chacha's cheeks lost most of their color as she saw by his look that Wishbone had more than half a mind to risk it. "Don't do it!" she cried, grabbing onto his arm. But Wishbone didn't even seem to notice her and said, "If you're willin' I should keep the Bullybueno horses you got a deal."

"Hell, I don't want your nags. I got all the horse I need right here in Giddy Joe. But mind, if you should back out, that's just the same as losin' and you'll sign the place over to me — understood?"

"Don't be a chump," Flack said. "This place'll fetch more'n that on the open market!"

But Wishbone said, "You got yourself a deal. Your fifty thousand against this ranch. Minus the horses."

And they shook on it.

Bixby, who had come up unnoticed, said, "Here's your winnings, Ashford, less the track's percentage," and handed over a couple handfuls of paper money, which Giddy Joe's owner stuffed into his pockets.

After Ashford had departed with his paint in tow, Bixby asked, "Left you pretty well strapped didn't it?"

"Oh," Reilly said, "I've still got close to ten thousand in the bank, and I'll have a heap more when we've run that race."

Bixby, eyeing him curiously, said, "I suppose it's possible. But to my way of thinking, you could be without a ranch in two weeks."

Reilly grinned. "Whyn't you look on the bright side? Rimfire thinks he's got a fix on that bad habit of Cat's. Look at the performance she put up today. She never slowed once till she was practically crossin' the line. In two weeks' time he'll have that all ironed out."

"You better hope so," Chacha said.

Chapter Twenty-Six

Chacha was feeling so bad about her filly's defeat and all the money Reilly had lost that she'd forgotten all about what the salesman from El Paso had left with her. Mightily upset by the crazy gamble Wishbone had made, she could hardly restrain herself from lashing out at him until they were in the house. "You should have had more sense than to have let him bamboozle you into it!" she cried.

Wishbone, sticking out his jaw, regarded her sullenly.

"You stood there like a stupid *paisano* and let him make a fool of you!"

"I don't know what you're yappin' about," he was finally moved to mutter, avoiding the accusing look she flung at him.

"Then what are you looking so guilty about?"

"I ain't lookin' guilty! What's more," he growled, "I'm tired of being nagged at. It's my ranch, damn it, and if I happen to lose it, it's no skin off your nose!" He slammed a big fist against the other opened hand. "I'm goin' to show that peckerneck where to git off at!" and storming into his room he banged the door behind him.

Although Wishbone refused to admit it, what she'd said had entirely too much truth in it. It was a drab and dreary prospect which despite all his bluster frightened him. He'd been a prize fool. He'd let that conniving rascal play him like a goddamn fish!

He could see it now just as plain as plowed ground. Ashford had let Chacha's filly win that first match and had almost allowed her to whip Giddy Joe a second time, baiting the trap cunningly to lure him into a third go. Then with his sneers and insults he'd maneuvered the heir to Bullybueno into dumping his inheritance into the pot. A slick and sneaky performance from first to last. His snare had caught Reilly beautifully.

Discovering this much, he could guess at the rest. No one had to hint to him whose hand was the hidden one back of this. It had to be Hannigan, and this was how that devil planned to get back at him! Foiled in his previous ploys, that bastard had come up with this means of ridding the ranch of its rightful heir.

Wishbone was hooked with no way to wriggle out of it, unless . . .

There was one slim chance.

He slipped out to the barn while Chacha was getting supper and buttonholed Rimfire.

"Do you think she can do it?"

Rimfire grasped straightaway what was in the boss's mind. "She can do it all right if she can just kick that habit. She's smart and has speed to burn. All she needs is to kick that quirk. I thought I'd got her out of it, made her want to be a winner. I dunno," he said and shrugged resignedly. "A habit like that is devilish hard to break."

"Would blinkers help?"

"I thought of that," Rimfire said, "but she'd still have ears, an' she knows how to use 'em. She plain don't like bein' out there by herself."

"We've got two weeks before that next match comes off. We better make good use of 'em, or you an me an' this whole damn outfit —"

"I know," said Reilly's half Navajo trainer.

"It's a hell of a responsibility I've saddled you with, but I believe in you, Rimfire — I believe you can do it. If we can show her how good it is to come in first . . ."

"Yeah," Rimfire muttered. "That's it in a nutshell." He rubbed a hand across his jaw. "Day after tomorrow I'll try her in blinkers."

"Nellie Bly's still around with Dalton's trainer. Get him to try her out against the Cat."

Dalton's trainer was agreeable. Two days later they loaded the pair into the stalls, sprung the gates and turned them loose for just a short work at 220 yards. Nellie Bly was the winner by about half a head.

Wishbone swore and Rimfire nodded. "She could play hide and seek with Nellie if she wanted."

"How long's her next work?"

"Four days from now I'll try her at 350."

"Run Potluck at her. Mebbe that'll make a difference."

The world took no notice of Whistling Cat's problem, although this second rematch was played up in the Tombstone papers and some that were much farther away, with several sidebars of comments pro and con by partisans.

Lum Fung, now the regular errand boy for Reilly, came back from town with another load of Horse Breeders letters with checks and cash, plus the suggestion the eat-and-drink stand should add hot tamales and chili to the next meet's menu. Chacha thought that was a pretty good notion, and Wishbone decided to do it.

The first and second night after Kitty's defeat an intensive scrutiny of the flowerpot couched among the canned plants on the eating room windowsill failed to disclose the least activity on the part of the elusive fly-catcher.

Considering the thing in disgust, Reilly said, "It's givin' this place a damn bad smell — prob'ly rottin'. If I was you, I'd heave it out on the manure pile where it belongs."

But Chacha, though eyeing it dubiously, still had hopes and refused to remove it.

One evening, well short of sundown, a pair of visitors from distant parts rode into the yard and were met by Jack Flack with a narrow-eyed stare.

"Lookin' for somethin'?" he asked coldly.

The older of the big-hatted strangers said yes, they'd come all the way from Chihuahua to have a look at the Bullybueno horses.

Flack yelled for Reilly; and Wishbone, with an eye to their sombreros, put on his best smile and invited them to dismount and rest awhile, which they were glad to do. "We understand," the younger one said, "you've horses for sale. We were told in Tombstone what you had were short horses — match-race prospects. We're anxious to obtain several of that kind. Could we see some?"

"You bet," Wishbone said, and to Flack, "Where's that last batch Rimfire fetched in?"

"Day pen. They been gentled enough you kin lead 'em around."

"Right this way, gents," Reilly said, leading the way past the bunkhouse and on toward a corral that held some two dozen horses. "These critters were mostly bred by my uncle, who was interested in what we call 'gamblers' horses."

The elder man said, "I am Esteban Ventura and this is my trainer, Emilio Arenas. I own the Hacienda Mila-flores near Mexico City. We were on a horse-buying trip in northern Chihuahua when we heard of the Bully-bueno horses and have come to see them for ourselves."

"We passed a two-lane track as we came in from the

gate," Arenas said. "Do you run match races here each week?"

"On Sundays," Wishbone said.

"From what I have read," Don Esteban remarked, "any person is welcome to wager, match, or simply observe. Is this so?"

"That's right," Reilly said. "If you can spare the time we'll be glad to put you up and you'll have a chance to watch these next matches. I mean, you'll see the way we do it up here."

"That would be most generous. I will try to rearrange our schedule to take advantage of your kindness."

They stood for a while by the corral considering the horses. Wishbone beckoned to Rimfire and explained when he reached them, "This is my trainer, Rimfire Jones. Don Esteban," he told the half Navajo, "is interested in match-race prospects."

Rimfire grunted and ducked into the pen, putting a halter on a big gray colt which he brought out and walked around for the visitors to look over. Arenas said, "They look fresh. How about that buckskin filly?" Rimfire nodded, put the gray colt back, fetched out the filly, and walked her around. After a moment Arenas, eyeing his *patrón*, said, "Let's see that blaze-faced dun."

This went on for about half an hour, Rimfire fetching out five or six more horses for the visitors' scrutiny. Then Arenas said, "What are you asking?"

Reilly said, "If you want more than one I could let them go at twenty-five hundred each."

The two men exchanged glances and Arenas said, "We'll take the gray colt, that line-backed buckskin, the *bayo coyote*, the *grulla* and that two-year-old *trigueño*."

After Rimfire made note of these in his dog-eared tally book, Don Esteban said, "I'll pay for them now and arrange to have them brought to my home in Mexico, if that suits your convenience."

Wishbone nodded and the money changed hands. "If it

would be possible," Don Esteban said, "I would be grati-
fied to see any horses you have in training, Don Tomas."

"You'll see them tomorrow," Wishbone said. And
Arenas asked, "Is it true you have agreed to race a cat
against that formidable horse Giddy Joe?"

Rimfire grinned and Wishbone explained, "It ain't a
cat really. What we've matched is a three-year-old filly
my housekeeper named Whistling Cat. We've got Joe
matched for three furlongs, not to run this Sunday but
the next."

"And is it true you have bet this ranch against Ashford's fifty thousand?" Don Esteban asked, looking prop-
erly impressed.

Scowling, Wishbone curtly nodded.

The *hacendado* said, "I should like to see this filly."

Wishbone's scowl grew almost as dark as the gathering shadows. Arenas asked, "Would you be interested in
selling her?"

"Not mine to sell. Belongs to Chacha Ronero, my
housekeeper."

Reilly's tone was so gruff no further questions were
asked. Rimfire went off in the direction of the barn as
the others cut over toward the house, which Flack, with
the dog on a rope, was just passing on his way to the
bunkhouse. Tantalizing supper smells made them quicken
their steps as Wishbone said, "About time for some grub
I reckon. Hope you gents have worked up a appetite."

Smiles lit the faces of the Mexicans.

It was soon apparent the Bullybueno housekeeper had
discovered she had guests. She'd put on her best dress
and a tiny apron and had fixed her hair in a way her
boss hadn't seen before. He thought she looked about as
pert as a little red wagon.

Flushed of face, she fetched in the food and, drawing
up chairs, the men sat down after Reilly introduced
Chacha.

She asked about their families and declared that she knew Don Tomas would want them to consider his house their own for as long as they could stay. After dinner, the men discussed horses over their coffee, and now and again Don Esteban was seen to be glancing about questioningly. Arenas, less tactful, wrinkled his nose. And Wishbone said, "It's that goddamn plant Chacha's wastin' her time on! Got the damn place smellin' like an assayer's shop!"

Rearing up with the napkin still in the neck of his shirt, he went hot-footing it over to the window, grabbed the flowerpot off the sill and, jerking open the door, heaved the offensive thing into the yard.

There was a blinding flash and a monstrous thunderclap. The whole room shook and everything in it seemed to jump and rattle.

Chapter Twenty-Seven

Reilly, flung backward, his arms outthrust, staggered but managed to stay on his feet. The guests, shocked, hung on to the table with white-knuckled fists while Chacha stared like an owl at her open-mouthed employer who gasped, "Gawd A'mighty! What in Christ's name was that?"

A babble of shouted questions came from outside, and the crew could be heard converging from the bunkhouse. Reilly, lurching to the open door, braced himself with a hand to each side and peered into the dark. Torchlight illuminated his face.

"Git that damn thing outa my eyes!" he bellowed.

Whoever was holding the torch swung the light away, and they all saw a gaping hole in the yard some fifteen feet beyond the veranda.

The guests and Chacha, crowding behind Wishbone, eyed the hole as if they'd never seen one before. Horrified at their narrow escape, Chacha cried: "Hannigan!"

"Damn right it's Hannigan," Reilly snarled, looking

like a trap-caught cougar. "He's the one put that pecker-neck up to this!"

"Blew that railin' clean off the porch," Horse Ketchum said with an admiring voice, and Rimfire allowed, "Be pickin' it up fer kindlin' halfway to Hayden!"

"Wonder," Reilly said, "it didn't take the porch along with it. What do you reckon was in that pot?"

"Well," Horse Ketchum said, drawing it out, "didn't seem to me it was any kind of a fly catcher."

Don Esteban and Arenas, with suitable apologies and many assurances of gratitude and friendship, took their departure the next morning as quick as breakfast was out of the way.

Rimfire threw his saddle on Kitty and began getting her ready for the race. Horse Ketchum and Flack, under Wishbone's direction, were beginning the task of filling up the hole when the deputy U.S. marshal rode up from the gate to stare in considerable astonishment.

"What you got there? Say, that ain't Cornelious's mine, is it?"

Reilly hawked up a good one and spat. When he got through cussing, he told the story of the obliging drummer and the gift of the flowerpot he'd left with Chacha.

"What'd this feller look like?" Bixby wanted to know. "Can you describe him?"

When Wishbone had done so the deputy said, "Sounds a heap like Yavapai Folsum. Not that you could prove it. When he wasn't cadgin' drinks he used to be a swamper at Rafferty's saloon. Probably dug for the tules the minute he left here."

"I say it was Hannigan put him up to it," Wishbone declared. "That bastard won't stop till he's rid this place of me!"

After turning it over in his mind Bixby nodded. "Expect you're right, but I see no way you'll ever pin it on him."

"Coulda blown the boss to Kingdom Come," growled Flack, "an' the girl along with him — not t' mention them Mex'kins!"

"Lookit the size of that hole!" said the Navajo. "You expect us to fill that in half a day? Take us that long just t' haul the dirt down here."

"You talk like a cowhand." Bixby grinned. "What they can't do from a horse is beneath 'em." He looked at Reilly. "What I come out this early for was to say it looks like you're bein' jobbed. Couple days ago I stepped into Rafferty's to wet my whistle, and who do you suppose I found off in a back corner with their heads practically touchin'?"

"Coulda been anyone."

"Well," Bixby told him, "it was Ashford and Hannigan."

"Ashford! Why, that dirty hound!"

"Makes a man think, don't it?"

Flack said, "A little tar and some feathers would do 'em both good."

"Never mind that," Wishbone said and swore. "What I'd like to know is what was in that pot."

"From your description," Bixby said, "the smell an' all, it's just about got to be some mixture of potassium cyanide put dry against silver paper in the bottom of the pot with mebbe two cupfuls of dirt coverin' it up. Long's it's kept dry, she's tame as a pet rabbit. All it needs to get a reaction is water seepin' down there."

"About a year ago," Flack said, "Hannah was powder monkey at the Lucky Cuss."

"Yes, well, he's huntin' holes these days to hide out in. Hannigan's the one that's pullin' the strings, probably cooked up this deal with Ashford soon's he heard you was buildin' this track; likely put up most of the money for the bet. Then Hannah comes up with this quicker solution. I'd like t' get my hands on that rascal! Reckon they want to get rid of you, Reilly."

"Hell," Reilly said, "I got onto that a good while ago. But you've sure enough opened my eyes to some other things. We're goin' to have to beat Giddy Joe or I'm done here!"

Bixby was staying over for the races tomorrow, but with so many other things camping on his shirttail, Wishbone didn't give a whoop about this next batch of races. He declared things had come to a pretty pass when a damn murderer like Hannigan was free to walk the streets rubbing elbows with him day in and day out.

"He's too sly to pull anything where we can get at him," Bixby said. "I got a halfway notion Hal Burton's afraid of him. Hannigan's not only slippery, he's a real sonofabitch with a pistol. Likewise he's careful not to do anything the town marshal, Earp, can latch onto him for."

At about this time they saw Chacha Ronero coming down from the house to see, no doubt, how Rimfire was getting along with her sprinter. When she arrived Wishbone said, "When did you water that damned flycatcher pot?"

"Well, I remembered the man said they didn't need much water, but since it didn't seem to be doing anything I thought a little water might get it started. So while you men were sitting there with your coffee I put a tablespoonful on it."

"You sure as hell got it started, all right. 'F I hadn't thrown it out, we'd be settin' right now with the heavenly host!"

She looked a bit upset, so Bixby hastened to say, "Never mind. Sooner or later somebody was bound to dump a little water in it. No harm done. Let's go see how the Cat is gettin' on."

"This last work was better," Rimfire told them. "She went three hundred and fifty yards an' led all the way."

"You run her against Potluck?"

"Yep, an' he tried his dangedest. I'll give her another work at four hundred about the middle of the week, and if she stays ahead in that one, I believe we've got it licked "

Chapter Twenty-Eight

He did, and she did too.

They ran her against Nellie Bly, who was a good solid performer up to four hundred yards, and Chacha's prodigy won by a length and a quarter. Her time was an even twenty seconds. This considerably impressed Bixby who, as an old match-race fan, had seen a heap of races.

"If she can carry that speed to three furlongs, I think you've a very good chance of beating Giddy Joe," he said. "Though Joe's mother was a pinto, he was sired by a Thoroughbred which means that in a sprint at this distance he probably has the edge. I very much doubt, however, he can go the first four hundred yards in twenty flat. That's really moving."

"At four hundred then," said Reilly, "she ought to be in the lead."

"If she don't ease up," Bixby said quietly.

Wishbone blew out a gusty sigh. "I reckon we'll just have to wait an' see."

Chacha said, looking wistfully at Reilly, "Oh, I hope she can do it!"

"You know," Bixby said, "it wouldn't surprise me a bit to find Hannigan in the crowd when the Cat next goes up against Joe. Now that we know Hannigan, Hannah and Ashford are in cahoots, it stands to reason Hannigan won't be leavin' more to chance than he has to. Since we're all agreed the prime thing he's after is to get you out of here, he's goin' to be on tap to make sure it happens.

"What I'm leadin' up to is you've got a watchtower with a bell in it. We better all be on the lookout, and if anyone spots him, get up in that tower and set it to ringin'."

"I got a better idea," said Wishbone nastily. "All the time that crowd's around we oughta have someone up there with a rifle, someone who knows how to use it!"

Bixby looked at him sternly. "Now just a minute. There's a word for what you're proposing. I'll admit there'd be no great loss if that rogue got himself killed, but I can't condone anything that smacks of dry-gulchin', Reilly."

"You're just splittin' hairs," Wishbone said sullenly. "If Hannigan shows it'll be for no reason but to turn me into a goddamn colander. I say a man's got a right to protect himself! An' doubly so when he's on his own property! He's come within a inch of killin' me twice."

"That's not the point. If you was to get up in that tower and squeeze a trigger soon's you got him into your sights, the law's goin' to call that murder, my friend, and sooner or later you'd swing for it."

"You'd never git a jury round here to say I wasn't justified three times over!" Wishbone snarled belligerently.

Bixby shook his head. "You can't do it, Reilly. I almost wish you could, but you got to give the man warning."

Back at headquarters Wishbone, still riled, hitched a

team to the wagon and, beckoning Chacha, told her to get aboard.

"Where are we off to?" she asked, settling herself beside him.

"Town," Reilly grunted, and kept his grim stare fixed straight ahead as they swept through the gate at a ground-thumping trot.

"Why have you put those disreputable clothes on?"

"Same reason I'm packin' this rifle."

She saw that he'd fetched along a couple of blankets, the sack of letters to be mailed and a pair of saddlebags as well. "I don't know what you think you're up to," she said, "but with our big race against Giddy Joe only two days away —"

"You'll find out when we get there. Now keep your mouth closed and both eyes skinned, an' if there's to be any shootin' you git flat on that wagonbed."

He'd picked the two fastest harness mules they had on the place and drove them like caisson horses, alternately walking and trotting them and where the terrain was easiest putting them into a ground-eating run.

They spent the night in the hills with twenty miles still to go. No fire. He dug into the saddlebags for jerky and biscuits, and these they washed down with water from the army canteen that had been banging against the side of the wagon.

Chacha wanted to talk, but he gave her no encouragement, being wrapped in his thoughts and answering only in grunts. They were off again before daylight, reaching town about nine, then leaving mules and wagon at Jack Crabtree's Lexington Livery Stable. The first place they visited was the sheriff's office. When Burton showed his surprise at seeing them, Wishbone came straight to the point and said, "Any chance of borrowin' you for a couple of days?"

"If it's important enough."

"It's important to us. We got a race meet scheduled at

Bullybueno. I'm expectin' trouble and I'd like for you to be on hand."

"Out of my jurisdiction. You already know that."

"I'm not askin' you to collar anyone. What I want's a impartial witness. One whose word'll carry some weight."

Burton considered him. "You share his conviction there's going to be trouble?" he asked Chacha.

"It certainly looks that way. Hannigan's shown he will stop at nothing in his attempts to get us out of there. Last week he tried to blow up the house," she said, and told of the spurious plant salesman, the flycatcher story and the flowerpot he'd left with them.

The sheriff, looking suitably impressed, admitted that was going pretty far. He told them that when they were ready to return he'd ride out to Bullybueno with them. "When do you plan to leave?" he asked, and Wishbone told him it would be inside the next hour.

They stopped by the post office and mailed their letters, picked up the few that were waiting in Reilly's box and walked around to the bank, where he changed the wording of his account to include the name of Earnestina Ronero. "I want it fixed so if I git shot she can draw what she needs or clean out the account."

When this was taken care of they went back for their wagon and went to Brown's, loaded some groceries and four big sacks of oats, then drove past the jail and picked up the sheriff, who set off with them on horseback.

Driving straight through they reached Bullybueno at ten that night, had a late supper and Burton went off to sleep in the bunkhouse.

The day of the big race dawned bright and fair, and the first thing on Reilly's agenda was a strategy session. Rimfire was left to his chores with the horses, but everyone else was fetched into the house and Burton asked Bixby what he thought of the prospects.

"I've no doubt there'll be trouble," Bixby said, frowning. "Hannigan's playin' pretty rough. He wants Reilly out of here."

"I can understand that," the sheriff said, "but trying to blow the place up seems a little excessive, even for a rascal of his stripe. How's he expect to get away with it?"

"Before Reilly inherited the place, he was running this spread like he honestly owned it, had possession and was patently ready to bury anyone with nerve enough to attempt to dislodge him. Besides, I guess he just figured that because this ranch is so far out the federal marshal wouldn't care what he did."

He told Burton of his conviction that both Ives Hannah and Ashford were in some way part of Hannigan's organization. "I think," Bixby said, "if Ashford looses this race, there'll be an all-out attempt to make buzzard bait of Reilly."

"And how do you propose to block this?"

"We've all got to keep our eyes skinned. There's a bell in that tower and if Hannigan's seen I want to hear it ring. If any one of those three yanks a gun out of leather, I think, in view of that blast, we'd be entirely justified in taking whatever steps seem appropriate."

And on that note the meeting broke up.

Chapter Twenty-Nine

Heading for the track, they saw that the early arrivals were out in force. There must have been at least 300 people milling around between the track and the stands, and a lot more were bellying the roped-off area east of the track. "Sounds like a bunch of wild turkeys gabbling!" Wishbone remarked. "Who's tendin' the gate?"

"Lum Fung," Flack said. "He'll collect, all right. He's got that old sawed-off an' a shut-tight box with a slot cut in it for the money."

"Good enough," Reilly said. "You'll be handlin' the food stand today," he told Chacha, "an' I don't want to see you outside of it till it's time for the big one. I'll send Horse Ketchum to fetch you to where I'll be at the startin' gates with Bixby. Burton will be at the track's far end to make sure there's no rough stuff at the finish." He took a quick look around. "Where's Good Eye?"

"Horse Ketchum's got him on a leash," Bixby said. "We don't want him runnin' out onto the track."

They saw Ashford approaching with Giddy Joe on a

lead shank. "Limberin' him up," Flack said, grinning.

The man went past without so much as a nod, Wishbone turning around to look after them. Whatever he was thinking he kept to himself. Bixby had stopped to have another look, too. "That shamblin' gait an' dropped head is something new fer Joe," the sheriff said. "You reckon he's ailin'?"

Bixby said, "It don't seem likely," but he kept on looking till they were lost behind the crowd. Burton asked Reilly, "You ever spend much time around your uncle?"

Reilly shook his head. "He was always off someplace lookin' for action."

"A pretty tough character," Burton commented. "Liked to gamble. Always on the move. Into one scrape an' out of another. Always wondered how he came to leave a feller like Hannigan in charge of his ranch."

"He didn't," Flack said. "I know that much. Hannigan simply moved in an' took over after the old man left on that last trip."

"Is that a guess?" Bixby asked.

"No guess about it. Tried to talk me into throwin' in with him." Flack snorted. "I didn't want no part of it!"

Wishbone asked, "You know anything about that mine Cornelious was supposed to have?"

"Heard rumors," Flack said. "Never saw any ore."

And Bixby said, "Didn't I hear that you worked for him once?"

"For about six weeks. That was all I could take. When things didn't suit him he was hell to be around."

"That lawyer at Hermosillo gave me to understand I'd inherited a mine along with the ranch; didn't seem to know much about it, though. Didn't know where it was. Told me Cornelious never recorded it. I been over this place with a fine-tooth comb. Do you suppose Hannigan knows where it's at?"

When Flack shook his head Wishbone asked, "About when was it he wanted you to throw in with him?"

"Three days or less after Cornelious left on that trip to Guadalajara. Had a hunch," he said, "the old man wouldn't be comin' back. Your uncle was always spinnin' big windies. Liked t' build himself up, make folks envy him. I don't believe he *ever* had any mine."

Reilly recalled the lawyer's words. "Great chunks of pure silver big around as washtubs." Big windies, sure . . . a lot of hot air.

And Burton declared, "That ol' man said a lot of things besides his prayers." Then, staring around, added, "Looks like you'll have a capacity crowd here today."

Bixby, looking off toward the gate, said "Biggest crowd ever."

Reilly, leaving the others, was on his way back to the house when, passing the refreshment stand, he pretty near stumbled over a one-legged beggar who was propped against it, tin cup in hand. About to stride past he stopped short, dug in his pocket and tossed a handful of coins into the cup for luck.

It wasn't until he was crossing the yard that it occurred to him to wonder how that fellow had gotten there. But with more important matters filling his head he went on to the corral and saddled up Rachel.

Looked like she was putting on weight standing around like she'd been these last couple of weeks. He had to thump a knee in her belly to get the trunk strap fastened. She peered round at him, reproachfully, as he swung aboard. He thought, setting off for the track again, he'd be a lot more likely to discover any enemies hidden in the crowd this way than he would afoot. Two in particular were pretty much on his mind.

He still hadn't seen them when he pulled up by the starting gates. Perhaps he was scuffing up a mountain from a mole hill. Hannah, anyway, wasn't apt to be found within reaching distance of a federal marshal, not with that Wells Fargo charge hanging over him.

The first race of the day went off without a hitch but was nothing to write home about, just a run-of-the-mill contest between a pair of cow ponies. Not much money was squandered wagering on these.

Wishbone rode his mule between the jostling throngs and on out to the end of the straightaway. There he jawed for a while with Sheriff Burton until the next race was being loaded into the gates. Then he backed Rachel off a ways to search the crowd. But he couldn't catch sight of the man he was looking for, the villain who was looming so large in his thoughts.

There were, by this time, crowds of gabby gesticulating people on both sides of the track. Not a great deal of money was changing hands, but a lot of new wagers were being shaped up. Reilly was halfway down the length of the track, setting back in the saddle still looking around, when a commotion broke out near the food stand.

Growls and a couple of truly ferocious barks were heard as Reilly thumped his heels against Rachel's ribs and made a beeline for the scene of the ruckus. Looking over the heads of those nearest, he saw Good Eye crouched with lips skinned back from gleaming teeth about six feet from a man who was struggling in the grip of several others to get his artillery clear of the holster. Wishbone caught one look at the man's distorted face as Bixby knocked the gun from his hand and hauled back his head with an arm locked under his jaw.

Still kicking and squirming, the man was trying to wriggle free when Reilly bent from the saddle and rapped his six-shooter against Hannah's head. Hannah went slack in Bixby's grip. "I want this bugger locked up," Bixby told those nearest, "until I've got time to deal with him. He's wanted for plenty, and I'm arresting him for taking mail and bullion off a Wells Fargo coach."

Reilly said, "I'll put him in safekeepin'. Couple of you boys hustle him up to the house. I got a closet up there he ain't goin' to git out of."

Wishbone stopped at the refreshment stand on his way back from seeing Hannah securely locked in the meat closet and making sure he was well guarded. Leaning from the saddle, he told a flushed Chacha over the heads of the hungry galoots trying to get her attention, "Soon's you've got these fellers taken care of I'll have Horse Ketchum fetch Good Eye over here an' you can lock up."

"Way you boss me around," she said to him tartly, "I bet you never had a housekeeper to order around before!"

"Hell," Reilly chuckled, "I never had a house before."

"And you'll probably never have one again after you get through betting what money you've got left on Kitty whipping that quick-healing Giddy Joe."

Wishbone peered at her. "What do you mean quick-healin'?"

"Two weeks ago that horse had a bad stone bruise across the front of his left hind hoof. Today I couldn't see any sign of it."

"You sure of that?" Reilly said sharply.

"Go look for yourself," she said, turning away to wait on the trade.

He rode over to where Bixby stood by the starting gates. "You put that varmint where he can't get loose?" the marshal asked, looking up at him.

"If he does, he's a wonder. When Ashford went past us with Giddy Joe this mornin' you turned clean around to look after him. Why?"

"I don't know really. Thought something about that horse seemed different. Imagination, I guess."

Reilly said grimly, "I had the same notion, and Burton thought he might be off his feed or somethin' the way he was shufflin' along with his head down, payin' no mind to anything. Two weeks ago when we run Kitty at him he had a stone cut across the front of that left hind foot. Today, he ain't got no cut."

Bixby, staring, said, "I'll be damned.

Wishbone finally said, "You reckon that swivel-eyed buzzard is fixin' to run a ringer in on us?"

Bixby said bleakly, "I'll damn sure find out."

Chapter Thirty

Chacha had sure enough given Wishbone some potent food for thought. Riding Rachel around he saw Horse Ketchum with the big shaggy dog at the end of a halter shank heading in the direction of the refreshment stand. Then he saw the one-legged beggar, but this time he was on two feet, yanking open the door. When the girl screamed, Wishbone was slamming the she-mule through the crowd without care, but Good Eye was a flying half dozen strides ahead of him.

When Wishbone flung himself out of the saddle, the dog already had the beggar down and was about to chew a good-sized hole in him when Reilly hauled him off. Horse Ketchum collared Good Eye as Wishbone jerked the man to his feet. There was blood coming from a gash on the man's neck and from a long scratch down one side of his face. When Lum Fung ran up with his sawed-off shotgun and the box with the gate receipts under one arm, Reilly shoved the mauled man back through the door with a growled, "Ride herd on him, Coosie," and turned to make sure the girl was still in one piece.

Turned out she was. She looked a mite pale, he thought, but all her parts seemed to be in working order as he shooed her out, called Good Eye inside and gave him a string of hot dogs to play with. "Take care of this place, boy," he told him and slipped out the door, shutting it behind him.

"You should have put the sides up," Chacha complained, but Reilly said in an offhand manner, "After that demonstration it'll take a pretty bold numbskull to open that door. C'mon — let's git over there," and catching hold of her hand, he shoved a passage through the crowd of gaping onlookers, closely followed by Horse Ketchum with the gate receipts, leaving Lum Fung to keep an eye on the phony cripple.

With ten minutes to starting time Rimfire was in his breechclout holding on to Whistling Cat near the stalls of the starting gates. Neither Ashford nor his pinto gelding were yet in sight, and Reilly looked at his watch and scowled. "You reckon," he asked Bixby, "that joker's run out on us?"

"By the terms of this match, I can't see him abandoning the money he's put up or losin' it by running out, not with Hannigan breathin' down —"

The rest of his words were lost because of the frantic banging of the bell in the tower. Unlike the people in the startled crowd, who were peering about questioningly, both men knew what that meant. Someone had spotted Wishbone's archenemy, and when the bell stopped its clamor, Wishbone, with a hand on his iron, was doing some peering around of his own. But the marshal, calm as a millpond, said, "He'll be savin' his spleen till after the race."

"I wouldn't give odds on it," Wishbone muttered, still searching the crowd with a narrowed stare.

"Unless the Cat wins, he'd be a fool to try anything. Here comes Ashford and the Cat's competition."

Amid jeers and guffaws Rimfire in his hot-weather garb leaped aboard Whistling Cat and reined her into the right-hand stall. But the horse under Ashford didn't want any part of that noisy rig and kept swerving away until Bixby, disgusted, grabbed the gelding's cheek strap and literally hauled the front half of him in. But that was as far as Bixby could pull him: The horse settled all his weight on his hind feet and wouldn't budge. Two handlers tried amid catcalls to shove him the rest of the way, but when it began to look as though they'd have to call the race off, two cowhands slipped a rope under his tail and he went in like he hadn't ever thought of resisting.

Giving him no chance for further antics, Bixby banged the tailgates shut and, yelling "Go!" yanked the release.

Whistling Cat burst into her lane as though she'd been shot from a canon. In seconds she was ahead by half a length. Passing the eighth pole she was leading by a length and seemed to be pulling away.

But before she reached the 350 marker it became obvious the paint was closing the gap. The Cat, Reilly thought, hadn't eased up a particle, but the paint was gaining with every jump.

At the 400 mark they were neck and neck, and then he began to pull away. From there on in it was apparent to everyone the Cat couldn't catch him, and he crossed the whitewashed finish line an easy winner by a length and a half.

The crowd was roaring itself into a frenzy when Ashford, standing in the stirrups, loped the big gelding back past Joe's vociferous fans on his way to the starting gates to pick up his money and the deed to Bullybueno.

But when he reached them, the triumphant grin fell from his face as Bixby said behind a leveled pistol, "Get off that horse. You're under arrest."

"Are you out of your mind?"

"That geldin' you're on ain't Giddy Joe, but a horse you fixed up to look just like him. You forgot the scraped place on Joe's hind hoof."

His face distorted with anger, Ashford cried, "You're not cheatin' me outa that win, by God!" His voice was half strangled with rage. "I won that race fair an' square —"

"You wouldn't know fair if it smacked you in the eye. Now get off that horse or I'll have you pulled off."

A ring of people twelve deep had gathered round them now. When Sheriff Burton clamped onto the spurious Joe's cheek strap, Ashford looked like a cornered rat. One of the handlers reached up from behind and, catching hold of his belt, yanked him out of the saddle, leaving him sprawled on the ground.

"Get him onto his feet," said the man from the U.S. Marshal's Office, coldly. "This rogue's due for a long stay at Yuma."

Then somebody said, "How d'you know that horse ain't Joe?"

"Anyone watching that race ought to know," Bixby said. "In the first match Joe was beaten. In the second he won by a nostril. You think Joe could win by a length an' a half? On top of all that this nag's got a hind hoof smooth as glass. Hang on to him, boys."

By this time Rimfire had brought the Cat up and looking down at them, said, "She was goin' all out when that ringer sailed past us."

"Joe never saw the day he could do that!" Chacha cried.

The crowd was slow to disperse after all this excitement and Bixby's announcement that all bets on that final race were null and void due to the fraud perpetrated by Ashford.

There'd been a lot of grumbling, but Bixby ignored it

all and herded his two prisoners up the lane in the direction of the Bullybueno ranch house. Lum Fung followed, his shotgun right behind the sullen-faced miscreants. Wishbone and Chacha brought up the rear, sort of lollygagging along, relieved by the knowledge they'd not have to lose Bullybueno after all.

"You ever noticed that most horses, unless you watch out, would just as soon step on your foot as not?" she asked as if that were the most important thing in the world.

"That's right," Reilly said. "Rest their weight right on it if you don't shove 'em off. Mules are smarter. You'd never catch Rachel bein' careless as that."

Looking up at him she said, "There's something I've been meaning to tell you. After that blast I found a crack in the wall. When he built the house, I don't think Cornelious put any foundation under it."

"I expect," Wishbone told her, "he just leveled off the ground. Most places round here are put up without foundations. We don't git any quakes around here and it sure ain't damp."

"You didn't let me finish," she said impatiently. "This crack, when I came to look close at it, was an up-and-down crack going clear to the floor; but at the top — about as high as my head — it went to the left in a sort of right angle — like a door," she said, "and that's just what it was. A hidden door shook loose by the blast!"

"Yeah?" Wishbone said, suddenly interested. "Did you get it open?"

"Well, of course. But there wasn't any knob."

"How'd you open it then?"

"I pried it open with that bowie knife your uncle had up on the wall over —"

"Never mind that," said Wishbone. "What was back of it?"

"A flight of steps, stone steps." She grinned at him. "Guess where they went."

"No place — house ain't got but one story."

"Well, they did. They went down to that mine you've been hunting for."

"By grab," Reilly said, and looked at her, speechless. "You're foolin'," he said finally. "You made it all up just to pull my leg."

"I didn't. It's there all right — you can see for yourself."

Wishbone slapped his thigh. "No wonder the old boy never recorded it!"

When they came into the yard, Bixby and the others were heading for the meat closet which someone had built onto the bunkhouse behind the kitchen. But Reilly steered Chacha into the house. "Show me," he said, and she led the way.

"It's right alongside the door to your office. I think Cornelious must have plastered it over."

"Funny I never noticed it," Reilly said, staring.

"You've been too busy to notice anything. Wait right here. I'll fetch that knife."

"Stay right where you are," another voice said. "Figured if I waited long enough you two would show up. Now turn around real slow an' get them hands up over your heads."

Wishbone guessed, before he turned, who he'd find there, and he was right. It was the black shape of Hannigan standing in the shadows with a gun in his fist.

Chapter Thirty-One

After all the risks and worries, all the contriving to get someplace in this sorry world, it all boiled down to a man with a gun. Of the handful of places one might have expected to see Hannigan, finding him inside Cornelious's house once more was the last thing Wishbone would have anticipated. Yet there he was, saturnine and ugly as a new-sheared sheep.

"I been a considerable while catchin' up to you, Reilly, but all's well that ends well, and this one looks to be all I could ask for. Get shucked of that iron, boy, *pronto*."

A good many notions flashed through the heir's head, but the odds were too clearly stacked against him. With thumb and first finger he delicately lifted his pistol from its holster. "Just drop it right there on that rug," he was told. He was awfully tempted to try some last minute heroics, but finally he let go of it.

"Now nudge it over here, boy." Hannigan grinned. "Nice an' easy."

When this was accomplished, a brief flexing of the knees allowed Hannigan to come up with it in his left hand. The grin turned even more sinister as he shoved Wishbone's pistol between his belt and belly.

"What happens now is goin' to make up for a lot of things, bucko. She's goin' to tie your hands with that rope over there. Then she'll get that door open an' we'll all go down for a look at that mine. Be a nice quiet place for you an' that slut with —"

That was too much for Reilly. Quick as lightning he sprang forward, with no regard for the gun. He smashed a rock-hard fist against Hannigan's jaw and, as the man reeled off balance, bashed him again. The gun went off. There were shouts outside, followed by the sound of running feet. Wishbone, overeager, came one step too close and Hannigan's knee caught him savagely in the groin.

Before he could straighten, the man had disappeared.

"Out the side door!" Chacha cried, and Reilly, scarcely able to catch his breath for the pain, lurched into the yard after him. He saw Hannigan disappear around the corner of the bunkhouse.

Reilly, still gasping, dashed for the barn, remembering Stegman's gun hanging just inside the door. Grabbing it, he spun around, looking for his foe. Guessing Hannigan was after one of the horses in the day pen, he cut around the nearest end of the bunkhouse and found Hannigan crouched and ready not twenty feet away. Hannigan fired twice as Reilly squeezed the trigger. The man, spun halfway around, crashed into a corral post, slid down it and was still.

Horse Ketchum hitched the team of mules to the wagon, and Hannah, cursing, was forced into it and then securely manacled to one of the side posts. Bixby charged him with taking mail and bullion from a Wells Fargo coach. Across from him, handcuffed to another post, was Ashford. Bound hand and foot on the bed between them lay the spurious cripple alongside Hannigan's cadaver. Half an hour later, with Bixby handling the reins and Lum Fung — who was to drive back the wagon — on the seat beside him, holding a sawed-off shotgun, they took off for town. Sheriff Burton rode directly behind on his blue roan with Bixby's horse on a lead rope.

Good Eye, sprawled on the porch, got up, tongue lolling out, to watch their departure.

"I gotta admit," Wishbone declared just before they set off, "justice works fast around these here environs."

"Well," Bixby chuckled, "it had a mite of help. It ain't a housekeeper you need, Reilly, it's a manager. Best advice I can give you is to marry the woman an' start raisin' heirs."

As he mounted the porch, Reilly smiled sardonically. He stopped for a moment then strode into the house, replaying in his mind Bixby's unasked-for advice. Matter of fact, for the past several days, whenever he wasn't worrying about losing the place, he'd been thinking along those lines himself. He found Chacha in the kitchen, bent over the stove, and before he could open his mouth she said, "I'll be leaving here Tuesday."

This stopped Wishbone plumb stiff in his tracks. "Leavin'! What for? Don't you like it here?"

"Of course I like it." She looked at him oddly. "Been kind of exciting when you stop to look back on it — too much excitement maybe. What I want's peace and quiet."

"Things'll be different now," he hastened to assure her.

"Anyway," she said, avoiding his gaze, "now that everything is settled you can keep this place without me nagging at you —"

"What kinda talk's that? I don't want you leavin'. What'll I do about meals an' all?"

"Lum Fung's a good cook. You can eat with the boys."

"Lum Fung wouldn't know a tamale from a tapadero. Hell, he wouldn't know a frijole from a firecracker! It's you I want, an' right where you're at!"

"You do?" She looked at him then, a funny expression on her face.

And Wishbone said, "I figured to have you round here permanent. Thought you knew that. It's what I asked you out here for. Once you got used to my rough ways it was in my mind you an' me would git hitched."

From the way her face lighted up he decided to throw caution to the wind. "Hell, you *will* marry me, won't you?"

"Yes," she cried, flinging her arms around his neck. "I thought you'd never ask!"

WAYNE D. OVERHOLSER

WESTERNS

FREE!!
BOOKS BY MAIL
CATALOGUE

BOOKS BY MAIL will share with you our current bestselling books as well as hard to find specialty titles in areas that will match your interests. You will be updated on what's new in books at no cost to you. Just fill in the coupon below and discover the convenience of having books delivered to your home.

PLEASE ADD $1.00 TO COVER THE COST OF POSTAGE & HANDLING.

- -

BOOKS BY MAIL

320 Steelcase Road E.,
Markham, Ontario L3R 2M1

210 5th Ave., 7th Floor
New York, N.Y., 10010

Please send Books By Mail catalogue to:

Name _____
(please print)

Address _____

City _____

Prov./State _____ P.C./Zip _____

(BBM1)